C.W. Allen

Tales of the Forgotten Founders

Published by: Cinnabar Moth Publishing LLC
Santa Fe, New Mexico

Cover Design by: Ira Geneve

ISBN-13: 978-1-953971-75-3
Library of Congress Control Number: 2023933426

Tales of the Forgotten Founders

C.W. ALLEN

CHAPTER 1
DUTY CALLS

"Protect the queen!"

Zed's eyes darted around in alarm as his grandmother's warning jolted him back to his senses.

"Quickly, we don't have much time!" Baba urged again.

What to do? Zed fumbled through his imagination, but every plan he came up with seemed less promising than the last.

"It's hopeless," his sister Tuesday declared. "She's completely surrounded."

But Zed wasn't ready to give in so easily. Things might look hopeless, but Baba of all people should know the power of persisting against the odds—they didn't call her the General for nothing. There had to be an escape route somewhere… or better yet, an opening to strike back instead of retreat. His eyes slid from the castle on the left, up to the front line.

Zed smiled. He'd spotted a vulnerability in the enemy's formation. If only he could get there in time…

An alarm blared, dissolving Zed's concentration. *No!* But that meant—

"Too late," Baba sighed. She switched off the timer and rose from the table to reset the chess board.

Zed had gotten so wrapped up in planning his attack strategy, he'd almost forgotten it was only a game.

Zed slumped back in his chair and looked around the spacious private library of his new home. It was the third place he'd called home in the last six months, and though he would have preferred a bit more stability in his family's living arrangements, he had to admit this one was a definite upgrade. Sure, the small suburban house he'd grown up in was cozy and familiar, surrounded by woods and only a short walk from a cheerful neighbor. The secret base he'd moved to next was far less cozy, but hanging out with a bunch of secret agents and their ingenious inventions had definitely been more exciting (especially when the base got raided by undercover soldiers.) But over the winter, his mother had inherited her childhood home, so his family had moved one more time. And this one was their best house yet because it wasn't really a house. It was a palace. Not a castle, exactly—the style was less Medieval European and more like the Greek-inspired buildings supported by tall white columns Zed had seen in fancy museums and banks. But that was just a technicality.

It wasn't perfect, of course. Palaces are almost always old, and their atmosphere often lacking in homey comforts.

Still, they do tend to come with certain perks, like private libraries. And that suited Zed just fine.

He was less excited about the reason his family had done all that moving around, but that could hardly be helped. It wasn't his fault his parents were fugitives from an alternate dimension. When rogue soldiers from that dimension decided to attack his normal, suburban house, the only way to escape had been for his family to move to Falinnheim, where his parents had been born. Discovering this had been enough of a shock, but then the rest of the story came out: Zed's mother was Falinnheim's last surviving princess. And now that the dictator who had wiped out the rest of her family had been defeated, that left Mom in charge of… well, *everything*.

Zed's attention turned to the chess board in front of him. This, too, was *almost* normal—and yet just different enough from the game he'd played back home to throw him off. The board layout and rules were basically the same as he'd learned in the school chess club last year. But instead of hollow plastic, the pieces of this set were heavy and solid, made from two different shades of hand-carved wood. Instead of folding cardboard, the board was made of interlocking squares of polished stone, white marble alternating with black volcanic rock. Strangest of all, this chess set had no bishops. Their places were filled by a pair of eerie ravens, their wings wrapped tightly around their carved bodies like winter cloaks.

"I almost had you that time," Zed told his grandmother as he collected the ravens and set them back into place beside the knights.

"No, you didn't," said Tuesday. She leaned in to give his king a flick, toppling the piece with a heavy *thunk.*

Tuesday was right, of course. Baba won every time. But even though his sister was two years older, she had never managed to beat their grandmother at chess either, so at least that was some consolation. Baba never went easy on either of them, and Zed chose to take that as a compliment. One of these days he was going to *earn* his victory.

To be honest, convincing Baba to come for a visit at all had been a kind of victory. Even when they'd lived together at the base, his grandmother had been far too busy for puzzles, or chess, or even a family dinner. Leading an underground resistance movement was apparently a round-the-clock responsibility. Now that Falinnheim's former dictator Tyrren was sitting safely in a jail cell, Zed had hoped Baba would have more time to catch up on all the grandmothering she'd missed during her duty as the Resistance General, but it seemed she was as busy as ever managing the new refugee resettlement agency. And she wasn't the only one, either. Mom was busy with princess duties, trying to straighten out the mess Tyrren had left behind in the sixteen bloodstained years of his takeover. Dad was leading the palace guard, attempting to sort out who could be trusted and which soldiers might still be hanging on to old loyalties.

Even his great-grandmother had a new job. Though Obaachan was nearly one hundred years old, she insisted she couldn't just hang around collecting dust—she had appointed herself to manage all the palace staff. And she was good at it, too. She was kind but firm and practical, and had a sharp eye for detail. No one ever argued with Obaachan. Especially not her daughter-in-law. Which is how after weeks of nagging, Obaachan had finally managed to talk Baba into visiting the palace for a bit of Grandma Bootcamp.

Things had been going... *okay,* so far. Two days in, and Zed and Tuesday already taken Baba on a tour of their new bedrooms, played a dozen games of chess, and even talked her into working on a jigsaw puzzle in the library while they ate lunch. The Royal Librarian, Gilford, hadn't seemed thrilled about letting them bring food anywhere near his precious books, but in the end he ran out of excuses to stop them. Maybe he figured with Baba there to supervise, they'd be less likely to make a mess. Or maybe he just couldn't work up the nerve to argue with the stern, silver-haired woman. Much like Obaachan, nobody argued with the General. And since only Zed and Tuesday were allowed to call her Baba, she was still the General to everyone else.

Suggesting a more friendly nickname for her grandchildren's use was about the only concession she had made so far, though. Zed knew she was trying, but she wasn't the cuddly sort of grandmother who baked cookies and told bedtime stories. After all, Baba hadn't even known she *was* a grandmother until his family's secret return to Falinnheim a few months ago—she'd spent over a decade believing her son was killed during Tyrren's takeover. The news that her son had escaped to another dimension with the princess he'd been assigned to protect—and then married her, and had a couple of kids in the meantime— must have come as quite a shock to a bitter, all-business resistance leader. A single week of Grandma Boot Camp probably wasn't going to change much, no matter how Obaachan tried to smooth things over.

Still… no way to know until he tried. "What's next?" Zed asked as he helped Baba return all the pawns to a straight line. "I bet if we went down to the kitchens the chef would let us use one of the workstations to make cookies."

"The kitchen staff will make cookies for you any time you want," his grandmother reminded him. "You don't have to make them yourself."

"Yeah, but wouldn't you rather make them ourselves? Not only to get a snack, but, you know… for fun."

Baba didn't respond. She just kept lining up chess pieces.

"Maybe we could teach Baba some games from home," Tuesday suggested. "We don't have the right equipment for video games or board games, but I bet we could find a deck of playing cards."

Baba appraised her silently for a moment. "But you *are*

home," she said at last. "You mean games from the *other* Earth."

"Sure, whatever," Tuesday answered. "Same thing." The conversation moved on, but Tuesday's thoughts lingered behind.

It was not the same thing at all.

In the end there was no point in arguing over what to do next—the schedule came to them. Their mother swept into the library just as the final chess piece was set back in place, but she barely had time to say hello before a massive shadow streaked past her and launched into Zed's chair.

"Ugh, Nyx!" Zed exclaimed, laughing and sputtering. "Get down!" He raised an arm to ward off the long, snuffling snout and slobbery tongue, but the enormous black dog carried right on licking his face. Zed knew he was fighting a losing battle. No one tells a Gabriel Hound what to do. No one besides Mom, that is. And on the rare occasion his mother felt the need to correct her pet's behavior, she could do it without giving a single command. Zed grew up assuming Nyx was playing favorites, or perhaps his mother simply had a knack for dealing with animals. It was not until the truth came out about his parents' links to Falinnheim that he learned Mom and Nyx could literally read each other's minds.

"Perfect timing!" his mother exclaimed when she saw that the chess match was over. "I was afraid I'd have to interrupt your game to get you there on time."

"Get us where?" Tuesday asked.

"To your dress fitting, of course. I told you about this at breakfast, remember?"

Tuesday made a face like someone had waved a sardine smoothie under her nose.

"Don't give me that look," her mother scolded. "The coronation ceremony is less than three weeks away. You can't show up looking like you've been playing hide-and-seek in a chimney. You're a princess now, and people will expect you to look the part."

Tuesday rolled her eyes. "*You're* the princess. The rest of us are just tagging along. It's your coronation—I don't see why it matters what *I* wear."

Princess Theadora might not have telepathic links to anyone besides her pet, but it didn't take a mind reader to know she meant business. And if Tuesday thought her grandmother might help her get out of this, a single glance at Baba was enough to squelch any hope of rescue. Mom and Baba wore identical frowns, and they were both folding their arms and doing the Mom Look.

"Come on Tuesday, it can't be *that* bad," Zed argued. "Just go and get it over with. Baba and I won't have *too* much fun without you, I promise."

Now it was Zed's turn to get blasted with the Mom Look. "Nice try, mister," said his mother sternly. "You've got an appointment with the tailor too. And you're about to be late, so get moving."

"Honestly," said Baba as she ushered Zed and Tuesday out the door, "I don't see what all the fuss is about. All you have to do is stand still for an hour or so. It's not like you're being tortured."

"Is torture an option?" Tuesday grumbled under her breath. "At least that would be exciting."

Everyone followed Princess Theadora out of the library and through the maze of hallways (some following more reluctantly than others) until they reached the tailor's workshop on the fourth floor. "When you're done here, head straight back to the library," she instructed. "Your new tutor is ready to start work—he asked you to meet him there. He said he wants to squeeze in a tour of the portrait gallery before dinner, so don't dawdle."

"But we're supposed to be hanging out with Baba this week!" Zed protested. "Can't school wait?"

"Look, I understand things have been hectic," his mother said patiently. "We've all been so busy getting moved in and starting new jobs… I've had to lead transition teams for both the palace staff and government officials, not to mention I have village councils from all over Falinnheim clamoring for my attention. Getting all the changes sorted out means you've been out of school for *weeks* already. If your tutor is ready to get started there's no reason to put school off even longer. You'll still have plenty of time to see your grandmother between lessons."

Zed wanted to argue that the opposite conclusion made

more sense—if several weeks out of school hadn't caused a problem, then surely a couple more days to enjoy Baba's visit couldn't hurt. But he knew there was no point. After all, Mom was a princess, and after the coronation she'd have some even fancier title. And if no one was allowed to argue with generals, or Gabriel Hounds, or even Obaachan, then talking back to the leader of an entire dimension wasn't likely to go very well.

Mom and Baba turned to leave, but Nyx didn't follow them this time. Instead she lay down and sprawled across the workshop's doorway, as if to block Tuesday and Zed from escaping.

"Isn't Nyx going with you?" Tuesday asked.

Her mother turned back with a sheepish expression. "Actually, that's why I came to get you myself instead of sending a messenger. I had a meeting with my advisors this morning, and a few of them claim they'd be more comfortable if Nyx didn't accompany me to all my appointments. Apparently, she makes some of the palace staff nervous."

"Gee, I can't imagine why," said Tuesday flatly. Nyx had just rolled on her back with her mouth hanging open, allowing her tongue to flop on the flagstone floor and exposing dozens of gleaming, dagger-sharp teeth.

"That's what I said!" her mother agreed, completely missing Tuesday's sarcasm. "But anyway, they all insisted it would be better if I gave Nyx some other job to keep her busy. After all, with your father in charge of palace security there's really no reason to have a Gabriel Hound for a bodyguard anymore. And you know Nyx never follows Dad's instructions, so I can't put her on patrol duty. But then I remembered what a fantastic job she did keeping you and Zed company when you first arrived in Falinnheim, so I decided we'd give that arrangement another try."

"*What?*" Tuesday yelped. "You mean we have to babysit a dog?"

"Don't be silly," said Baba as she continued up the hall. "The dog is babysitting *you.*"

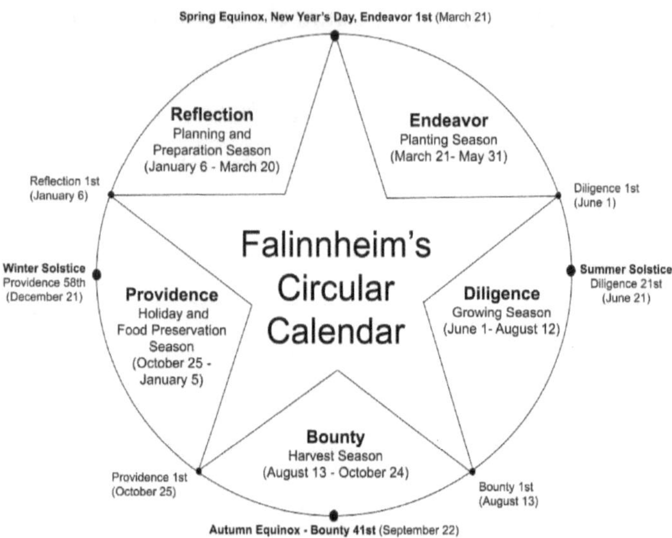
Spring Equinox, New Year's Day, Endeavor 1st (March 21)
Reflection
Planning and
Preparation Season
(January 6 - March 20)
Endeavor
Planting Season
(March 21- May 31)
Reflection 1st
(January 6)
Diligence 1st
(June 1)
Winter Solstice
Providence 58th
(December 21)
Falinnheim's
Circular
Calendar
Providence
Holiday and
Food Preservation
Season
(October 25 -
January 5)
Diligence
Growing Season
(June 1- August 12)
Summer Solstice
Diligence 21st
(June 21)
Bounty
Harvest Season
(August 13 - October 24)
Providence 1st
(October 25)
Bounty 1st
(August 13)
Autumn Equinox - Bounty 41st (September 22)

CHAPTER 2
THE TAILOR AND THE TUTOR

It wasn't quite an hour, and it wasn't quite torture. But Tuesday was pretty sure having to stand perfectly still for her dress fitting came close on both counts. And anyway, it wasn't so much the process she objected to. The real insult, in her opinion, was that an entirely new dress was being made from scratch, and she got absolutely zero say in how it should look.

"A nice bright green, don't you think?" the tailor said as he alternated between surveying Tuesday and the bolts of fabric lining the walls of the workshop. He selected a bolt the shade of radioactive pond scum and held it up to Tuesday's face, though how he managed to test it against her complexion while completely missing her contemptuous expression was anyone's guess. "Such a feminine shade, and perfect for a New Year's Day coronation—it's the color of the Endeavor season, after all!"

"I thought pink was supposed to be the girly color," Zed commented from the corner, where the tailor's apprentice was busy taking his measurements.

"Pink?" said the tailor absently as he flipped through his pattern book. "Why pink?"

Zed had never really thought about it before. "I dunno, it just seems like stuff for girls is always pink. Or sometimes purple. Or pink and purple together."

"Nonsense," the tailor mumbled back, his mouth now full of pins as he draped the fabric over Tuesday's shoulder and tacked some pleats into place. "Everyone knows green is for girls. It's tradition, and upholding tradition is especially important at a coronation. People want to feel a sense of stability going into a new era of leadership."

"It's perfect," said Tuesday, her voice dripping with disgust. "I've always wanted to stand in front of an enormous crowd dressed like a frog."

"Okay, then," Zed tried, "if green is for girls, what color is for boys?"

"Yellow, obviously," the apprentice cut in.

"Why, though?"

"Who cares!" Tuesday interrupted. "The whole thing's stupid. Why should colors matter at all?"

"You're quite right," said the tailor. "Besides, yellow wouldn't suit Zed anyway, it would clash with the warm tones in his hair. No, I was thinking of a nice rich eggplant shade. Or maybe plum? The plum is a slightly redder purple, but I prefer the texture of this eggplant brocade…”

By this time Zed and Tuesday had both tuned out; they decided to play along and get the fitting over with. After a mind-numbing eternity of holding their arms out like scarecrows and rotating slowly while hem lengths were marked, the tailor finally said they were free to go. This was easier said than done, because when they headed for the exit, they found Nyx had fallen asleep sprawled across the threshold, barricading the doorway and snoring like a hibernating bear.

Zed nudged her with his foot. “Come on, Nyx. Time to go.”

The dog carried right on snoring.

Tuesday hadn’t been thrilled with the idea of constant supervision by someone with a direct link to her mom’s brain, so she decided this was an excellent opportunity to give her canine chaperone the slip. She tried to quietly step over the sleeping mass of black fur, but Nyx chose that exact moment to roll on her back, stretching her long, spindly legs in the air and forcing Tuesday to hop backwards on one foot to avoid tripping into her.

The snoring got louder.

Zed was just debating whether it was safe to rouse Nyx more forcefully, or if this might startle the Gabriel Hound into unexpected flames, when he heard a slight rustling noise behind him. The tailor’s apprentice pulled a wad of waxed paper out of her handbag and unwrapped it to reveal a leftover gooseberry muffin from breakfast.

Nyx's ears perked up. Her eyes shot open. Before anyone could register what was happening, Nyx was nothing but a dark blur whooshing between Tuesday and Zed. The apprentice didn't even have time to panic; she just blinked down at her now-empty hand, wondering where her afternoon snack had gone, while Nyx licked crumbs off the floor.

Tuesday rolled her eyes, grabbed Zed's arm, and headed for the door.

———

They made their way back to the library, the clicking of Nyx's toenails echoing off the stone floors with every step. But when they arrived, the only person inside was the librarian, Gilford. The stern middle-aged man peered at them from behind the ancient, threadbare cover of the book he was reading, closed it with an irritated sigh, and stood from his desk in the corner.

"Must that beast come with you everywhere?" he asked, wrinkling his nose in disgust when he caught sight of Nyx. "This is a library, not a petting zoo."

"Sorry," said Zed. "Mom's orders."

"Trust me, we're *way* more annoyed by this arrangement than you are," Tuesday added.

"We won't be here long, anyway," Zed assured him. "We're just meeting our new tutor here, and then we'll be out of your way. Whoever it is, they should be here soon."

"Your tutor is already here," said Gilford stiffly, smoothing his graying, pointed goatee.

Tuesday scanned the rows of dark wood bookshelves and reading nooks clustered with velvet sofas. Dust particles danced silently in a sunbeam streaming in from a bank of arched windows that formed one entire wall of the room. The library seemed deserted except for the three of them.

"*I* have been placed in charge of your education," Gilford clarified. "It's tradition for the Royal Librarian to serve as private tutor to the children in the palace household, although up until now that hasn't been an issue."

"Because there weren't any kids living here before we moved in?" Zed guessed.

"Not exactly. There is one other child in the palace, but my last, ah… *employer* preferred I attend to him during my personal time, rather than as an official duty. Now that things are different…"

Gilford paused uncomfortably.

Zed was pretty sure he knew what had the librarian bothered: the last person to call the palace home was Tyrren. And since the former dictator had a habit of making anyone who annoyed him "disappear", Zed imagined all the palace staff had been working under rather stressful conditions.

"Well, let's just say things are different," the librarian

concluded. "We have enough students for a real class, so that is what we will do."

"Where's the other student?" Tuesday asked.

"Late," said Gilford.

Several minutes dragged by, which Nyx decided to fill by settling in on one of the (probably extremely antique) sofas and licking her paws. When she decided her paws were clean enough, she moved on to licking the upholstery underneath them, which made the librarian grind his teeth. Finally Gilford couldn't take it anymore and announced they'd be starting their tour of the portrait gallery without waiting for the third student.

"I can't imagine where that boy's gotten to," Gilford muttered under his breath.

———

The portrait gallery was exactly what Tuesday had expected: a long, echoing hall lined with life-sized paintings of people in old-fashioned costumes who all looked like they had toothaches. Nyx trotted along beside them, scanning the hall for interesting scents while the librarian began his tour.

"You are in a unique position as students," Gilford lectured as he led them through the gallery, namedropping each of the famous portrait subjects they passed as though he was bragging about knowing them personally. "Most children your age already know all about Falinnheim's history, geography, and culture, so you have a lot of catching up to do."

"So," Zed ventured, "if you know we've missed out on all that stuff… I guess that means you know about the other Earth?"

Gilford raised an eyebrow at him. "Princess Theadora filled me in on the basics, yes."

"Does that mean we don't have to keep it a secret anymore?" Tuesday asked.

"No—"

"No, it's not a secret, or no, it doesn't mean that?" Zed interrupted.

"Princess Theadora can share classified information with whomever she deems necessary," Gilford said, drawing himself up importantly. "*You*, on the other hand, cannot."

"Figures," Tuesday grumped. "We helped take down an entire dictatorship, but we still get treated like kids."

"We *are* kids," Zed reminded her.

"Hey, whose side are you on, anyway?"

Gilford ignored the interruption and carried on with his lecture.

"In order to make a lesson plan, I needed to understand the gaps in your previous education, and apparently those gaps include Falinnheim's entire history. However, you do have one advantage: unlike most students, you have a personal connection to the people and events we will be studying." Gilford paused to admire a painting of a sour-faced old man dressed in gold-embroidered robes. "Take this portrait, for example. Octavian the Calculating ruled Falinnheim over six hundred years ago. That makes him your twentieth great-grandfather. We even have a few artifacts from his reign in the palace vault. As the youngest generation of the royal family, you are the only two children in the world who can claim that heritage."

Tuesday frowned skeptically up at the man's painted features. "What was he famous for? Was he some inspirational leader during a crisis, or something?"

"Well, you're half right," said Gilford. "He was a leader during a crisis, and his influence definitely changed the course of Falinnheim's history. But that's because he *caused* the crisis. Octavian the Calculating was the last emperor of Falinnheim. He's the reason the Regents Council was created, in fact. You see, Octavian secretly poisoned most of his relatives so he could inherit the throne."

"He sounds charming," said Tuesday sarcastically. "Can't tell you how thrilled I am to be related to him."

"What's that got to do with the regents?" Zed asked.

"The records are a bit fuzzy on how the poisoning was discovered," said Gilford. "It's possible everyone knew about it at the time, or at least suspected, but no one had the power to do anything about it. Years later, Emperor Octavian's children agreed this system of passing total control to a single heir when the previous ruler died created a horrible incentive for murderous plots, so they decided Falinnheim couldn't have an emperor anymore.

They designed the post of Moderator with the opposite rules: all members of the royal family get a lifetime appointment to the Regents Council at the age of twenty, with the oldest member of the clan serving as Moderator. The Moderator acts as an experienced counselor to the other regents but is no longer a voting member of the council. That way, there's no incentive to speed the inheritance process along."

Zed had learned bits and pieces about Falinnheim's system of government before—at least, what it used to be like before Tyrren took over and messed everything up—and it seemed like a sensible enough arrangement. Sure, he was used to things being run a bit more democratically, but as monarchies went, this Regents Council arrangement sounded pretty clever. But he'd never really thought about how things got to be that way. Not Murdering Your Relatives didn't strike him as the sort of behavior that should *need* any incentive.

They came to the end of the hall. The last painting showed a bronze-skinned young man posing with a weird contraption that looked like a cross between a wagon wheel and a toy sailboat. His face was flecked with freckles and framed by dark red curls—an unusual combination, Tuesday thought. Most redheads she'd seen before were ghostly pale. Tuesday stepped back to appraise him for a moment, wondering if this man might be a distant ancestor too, but then something at the edge of the portrait caught her eye. There was a round, shiny object on a side table next to the man's chair, almost out of frame. She moved closer and squinted at it. It had a warm metallic finish, and she thought she could make out a faint seam across the middle. It almost looked like… a compass. Like the one Scrimbley had used to bring her to Falinnheim in the first place.

"Who is this?" Tuesday asked.

"Ah, that's Julian the Tinker," Gilford explained, smiling fondly at the ancient painting as though he was introducing an old friend. "Third emperor of Falinnheim. In addition to his leadership during a rather severe blizzard one Reflection season, Julian was also known for his inventions. He developed a new timekeeping device that improved on sundials but came before mechanical clocks."

"But he invented other things too?" Tuesday pressed.

"Probably," said Gilford. "The timepiece is the one he's most known for, but—"

Tuesday interrupted him. "Would any of Julian's artifacts be in the palace vault?"

"I seriously doubt it. Julian lived over a thousand years ago. The portrait itself is artifact enough, and some art scholars believe it may have been painted after his lifetime anyway."

"You said he was the third emperor," Zed pointed out, "but it's the last painting. Who was in charge before that?"

"Well as I said, this was over a thousand years ago. We have a few more names going back in the written records, but there are no paintings of the early rulers. It was simply too long ago."

A plan was brewing in Tuesday's mind. She wanted to ask Gilford more about this vault, but at that moment Julian's painting swung out from the wall like a door, and a face emerged along the edge of the frame.

Startled, Tuesday jumped back. The painting eased forward on hinges hidden under the left side of the frame and a lanky teenage boy stepped out from a shadowy passage behind the wall. His dark brown hair was just long enough to brush the collar of his button-front tunic, and he wore a lopsided, mischievous smile that wouldn't have looked out of place on a fairytale imp.

Nyx dashed forward to greet the new arrival, planting her front paws on his chest and slurping his chin.

"I wondered when I'd get to meet the famous Gabriel Hound," the boy said, playfully mushing Nyx's ears around.

"Bastian!" said Gilford in exasperation, "Where have you been? You were supposed to report for class half an hour ago. You've completely missed the portrait gallery tour."

"I thought you said to meet you here," the boy answered carelessly. He heaved Nyx's paws off and rubbed his face against one arm to wipe off the dog slobber.

"I said no such thing. You never li—" Gilford caught himself and let out a breath to reset his composure. "My nephew, Bastian," he told Zed and Tuesday, by way of introduction. "He's fourteen, so he has a year left before choosing an apprenticeship. In the meantime, he'll be joining us for classes."

"Great-nephew, actually," Bastian corrected. "But thanks for the invite, Uncle Gil. Not that I had a say in this arrangement, or anything. But it'll be nice to have some company closer to my age for a change."

"Are you really the only other kid living in the palace?" Zed asked.

"Yup. My mom works in the village liaison office and my stepdad is the palace hoversled mechanic, so we've lived here for years. Sometimes the chef or the stable master or somebody had a teenage apprentice, but they were always older than me, and busy working anyway."

"And now that you're not my only pupil," said Gilford sternly, "you'll need to learn more consideration for your fellow students' time."

Bastian shrugged and shot the librarian a sunny grin. Gilford glared for a moment, then walked briskly around the corner to the next hallway as though there had been no interruption. "Come along, everyone," he said over his shoulder. "We have just enough time to view the palace sculpture collection before dinner."

"So what's with the hound?" Bastian asked as they followed Gilford. "I heard it was supposed to guard the Princess. One of the linen maids claims they're together every moment of the day."

"Nyx used to do that," Tuesday explained, "but

apparently some of Mom's advisors are scared of her, so now Nyx has to hang out with us instead. She's supposed to keep us out of trouble, I guess. Not that we'll have time to get into trouble, between your uncle's classes and all the coronation stuff going on, but whatever."

"Huh," said Bastian, laying a hand on Nyx's back as she trotted along beside him. "So instead of your mom having a dog for a bodyguard, now you've got a dog for a nanny." He laughed. "It's like something straight out of *Peter Pan*!"

It took Zed a moment to register what Bastian had said. "Wait a minute…" he whispered as the realization settled in. "How do *you* know about Peter Pan?"

CHAPTER 3
WELCOME TO THE BUNKER

Bastian checked over each shoulder as though making sure they weren't being followed (which was a bit over the top, Zed thought—the corridor was clearly deserted except for Gilford, who was nearly an entire hallway ahead of them by this time). He leaned in close and whispered to Zed. "*You* know about Peter Pan?"

"Sure," Zed answered, "he's a character from an old book. Well, actually it was a play first, but there was a novel version later, and then a bunch of movies, and—"

Bastian put a finger to his lips, silencing Zed's explanation. Then he doubled back to the portrait gallery and re-opened the door covered by the final painting. "Come on," he said, "I want to show you something."

Tuesday, Zed, and Nyx followed him into the dark opening behind the painting. The moment Tuesday pulled the frame closed behind her, rows of crystals set into the walls glowed to life, revealing a long, straight, stone corridor. Though it was twice as wide as a typical door frame, the ceiling wasn't any taller, so even though they could all stand upright with room to spare, things felt a bit cramped.

"It's not far," Bastian assured them, leading the way up the passage.

"Any second now, Gilford's going to notice we're not following him anymore," Zed pointed out, his whisper echoing off the surrounding walls.

"Oh come on," Bastian argued with a wink, "We've got a couple dozen seconds, at least. Besides, Uncle Gil just likes hearing himself talk. He'll keep blathering on whether he's got an audience or not."

They walked in silence for only a minute before Bastian stopped. He selected one of the stone blocks of the wall and pushed it in as though pressing a massive button. The block sank into the wall a few inches, and then all the blocks surrounding it swung inward on hidden hinges to form a recess set into the middle of the wall like an oversized window.

"After you," said Bastian, grinning.

They stepped over the parts of the wall that hadn't moved, through the dark hole, and emerged into a square, windowless room. Like the passageway outside, the walls, floor, and ceiling were made of gray stone blocks with a row of light crystals embedded halfway up the wall. The crystals lit themselves automatically when Bastian closed the disguised door behind them.

"Welcome to the bunker," said Bastian proudly.

Normally, Tuesday made it a point not to seem too impressed by anything, especially not anything her little brother got excited about. After all, she was almost thirteen—only one week to go—and teenagers had seen enough of the world to take new developments in stride. *Two* worlds actually, in her case. But for the moment, it was all she could do to prevent her eye sockets from sprouting little cartoon hearts. She just stood there next to Zed, staring around in amazement, drinking in the realization: she lived in a real-life ancient castle! With secret passages behind the paintings! And a hideout so double-secret, it had its own hidden entrance *inside* an already-hidden passage! Nobody, absolutely nobody, was too cool to appreciate this.

Nyx took a lap around the spacious room, nose to the ground, inspecting everything. In one corner, a mound of mismatched throw pillows formed a makeshift seat. A colorful flock of torn kites and overturned umbrellas hung from the ceiling. A dozen small delivery crates were stacked on their sides along the next wall like a shelving unit, their compartments clustered with cracked vases, chipped teacups, and other castoff supplies.

"Tuesday and I used to hang out in a treehouse," Zed volunteered. "You can't exactly *hide* a whole tree, though. A secret hangout with its own hidden passage is way cooler."

"Oh, you haven't seen anything yet," Bastian assured him. "There are hidden doors and passages all over the palace! The bunker is the best one though—the staff knows about most of the others. That's the whole point of the passages, so the servants can get around the palace quickly and do their jobs without bothering anybody. Hiding the entrance to a secret room inside a secret passage is pretty genius, though. If anyone other than the palace staff happened to find the tunnel behind the painting, they'd be so proud of themselves for discovering it they'd never be on the lookout for *another* disguised door. And anyone who already knows about the passages is busy using them to deliver meals or collect dirty laundry or whatever, so they never bother to explore."

"It's perfect," Zed agreed. "Good thinking!"

Bastian laughed. "Well, it's not like I built the secret room myself. I just got bored enough to find it a few years back, that's all. I grew up without anybody else to play with, so it's almost like the palace itself became my friend, you know?"

Tuesday shook her head to dislodge the wonderstruck look from her face. *Focus, Tuesday! There's a mystery going on, remember?* She cleared her throat. "This is really great and all," she told Bastian, "but can we get back to the point? Zed's right, you're not supposed to know about stuff from the other Earth. Where did you hear about Peter Pan?"

"Listen, everyone's heard the rumors," Bastian explained. "For years people wondered if some of the royal family might have gone into hiding—maybe on one of the Outland Islands or something. But once the Princess made that dramatic entrance at the Solstice parade, the gossip mill started working overtime. People said the only way the missing regent managed to avoid Tyrren's spies for so long was to hide out somewhere so secret, only the royals even knew it existed. And suddenly, some things I'd read as a child started to make a lot more sense. I realized she must have found someplace like Neverland or Oz."

Tuesday and Zed exchanged dubious looks. If any place counted as a secret fantasy land, it was Falinnheim; the rest of the Earth was the normal, boring part. But apparently Bastian didn't see things that way.

Bastian sifted through the collection on the crate shelves and gathered up a stack of books and papers. "I'm probably not supposed to have these," he said, though he didn't sound the slightest bit guilty about having them anyway. "I found them in a trunk of my great-grandma's stuff after she died. Normally, old books are Uncle Gil's department, but since they're children's books he didn't want them for the library. He probably would have thrown them away if I hadn't snuck them out of the trunk. And the rest of it looked like useless junk to begin with."

Tuesday took the stack from Bastian and sat down on the floor to look through it. The books were in pristine condition, but she could tell from the linen covers and embossed lettering that they must be fairly old. *"Peter and*

Wendy. The Wonderful Wizard of Oz. The Jungle Book. Grimm's Fairy Tales…" Tuesday looked up at Bastian, perplexed. "These books are all from the other Earth! Why would your great-grandma have them?"

Bastian just shrugged. Nyx, having finished her inspection of the room, sat at his feet and looked up at him until he got the hint and resumed scratching her ears.

"Remember when we first met Scrimbley?" Zed asked.

Tuesday rolled her eyes. "How could I forget? It's not every day you get attacked by sword-wielding weirdos, your dog goes up in flames, and your treehouse turns into a portal to another dimension."

"Wait, what?" Bastian interrupted. "I have *got* to hear that story."

Zed ignored him. "Not that part… I mean the part where Scrimbley explained about his compass transporter thingy. He said it had been hundreds of years since Falinnheim was in contact with the rest of the world. That's the only reason Mom's code worked—because she knew no one in Falinnheim would have heard nursery rhymes before."

"Yeah, and?"

"These books may be old, but they're a lot newer than nursery rhymes." Zed sat down next to Tuesday and started flipping through the covers. "*Grimm's Fairy Tales* looks like the oldest one here. The copyright page says 1823, but this edition could have been printed later, I guess…"

Tuesday dug through the rest of the collection. Bastian

was right: it sure looked like junk. The label from a can of creamed spinach. A water-stained old magazine. A slightly squashed paper airplane. A blank postcard from some beach resort she'd never heard of. But then she got to the last item.

"Look at this," she said, passing her discovery over to Zed.

It was a small poster with a stack of even-smaller pages stapled to it. The top half featured an illustration of a girl in a ruffly white dress sipping from a glass cola bottle through a straw. But it was the bottom half of the poster that made Zed stare.

Below the picture was a calendar, showing the dates for March.

March, 1918.

Zed flipped through the tacked-on pages. April, May, June, July… all the way to December, every page showed dates for 1918.

"How old would your great-grandma have been in 1918?" Zed asked Bastian.

"Ah, well—see, that depends." Bastian gave Nyx one last pat and crouched down to join the others on the floor. "What's… nineteen-eighteen?"

Zed knew Falinnheim used a different calendar system than he was used to, which started each new year at the spring equinox and divided it into five seasons. But he'd never given any thought to how the years were numbered. Apparently Falinnheim did things differently. "This is a calendar," he explained, passing it over for Bastian to examine. "1918 is the year it was printed, which was more than a hundred years ago."

Bastian's face practically glowed with delight. "I *knew* it had to be a calendar!" he said, ignoring Zed's question. "The days of the week are the same, but I couldn't sort out the rest. Seems pretty complicated, if you ask me." He flipped through the pages. "Ten seasons instead of five, then?"

"They're called months," said Tuesday, "and there are twelve, not ten. The first two pages are missing from this calendar."

Bastian looked through the stack again, looking perplexed. "The *first* two? You're sure the extra months don't belong at the end?"

"Of course I'm sure," Tuesday huffed.

"It's just… when I thought there were only ten, it made more sense. See October, here? *Oct* means eight, doesn't it? Like in octopus or octagon. But if two months are missing from the beginning, that makes October the tenth month, not the eighth. And these others are numbered, too: *Sept* for seven, *Nov* for nine, *Dec* for ten. Why would a calendar name months after numbers, but put them in the wrong order?"

"Hey, it's not like Zed and I invented it," Tuesday argued. "That's just the way things are."

Bastian shrugged. "Not around here, it isn't."

Zed tried to get the conversation back on track. "The point is, using this system you need a new calendar every year. And this one says it's over a hundred years old. Where would your great-grandma get something like that?"

"Beats me," said Bastian. "She only died five years ago, and I think she was around ninety at the time. She wouldn't even have been born yet when this was new."

"And it's from a world no one in Falinnheim is supposed to know about, let alone be collecting souvenirs from," Tuesday added.

"Your mom found a way," Bastian pointed out.

"True," said Zed. "And apparently, she wasn't the only one."

CHAPTER 4
CLASS DISMISSED

Gilford paced through the forest of black stone pedestals. "Where in Hades' Hairnet could those children have gotten to? I turn my back for thirty seconds, and—*AUGH!*" He startled backwards, nearly toppling the nearest statue, when he caught sight of a pair of glowing eyes shining eerily from the shadows of the massive fireplace on the opposite wall. Nyx slunk out of the space that would have held flaming logs if the fireplace had been lit, followed by three grinning, slightly sooty kids. There was a scraping sound as the blocks forming the back wall of the firebox slid back into place, covering the hidden passageway beyond it.

"Bastian!" Gilford scolded, trying (and mostly failing) to sound as though watching his delinquent students emerge from the depths of the fireplace was a normal, everyday event that hadn't caught him off guard in the least. "Where have you three been?"

"We took a shortcut," Bastian replied with a wink at Zed and Tuesday.

Nyx shook herself from scruff to tail, her back paws doing a tiny tap dance against the slick marble floors as she removed the last bits of ash from her coat.

"The only thing getting cut short around here is my patience," Gilford retorted. "Now please, no more wandering off." And with that, he launched into his lesson on the palace's sculpture collection.

"What do you think they're serving for dinner tonight?" Bastian whispered to Tuesday as he tried to look thoroughly engrossed in Gilford's explanation about the bust of Aldous the Fanciful. "I hope Maisie's doing another batch of those garlic butter popovers, those were amazing."

"Perhaps you'd care to share your comment with the rest of us," Gilford cut in, eyeing Bastian sharply.

Bastian nodded. "I was just mentioning the cross hatching on this sculpture. I really like how the artist's use of texture highlights the contrast between the sculpture's realism and the subject's personality."

Gilford blinked. "Yes, that's an excellent point," he said at last. "I'm pleased to see you're paying attention, for once."

"Always, Uncle Gil."

The librarian returned to his lecture, which was Bastian's cue to shoot Tuesday and Zed another wink.

———

Just when Tuesday was beginning to doubt Gilford

would ever run out of things to say about art, and history, and art history, the librarian announced the class was dismissed. "We'll meet in the library immediately after lunch tomorrow," he called while his students filed out of the room (through the door, this time). "There's a fascinating collection of old maps I'd like to discuss."

Bastian scritched Nyx's ears as he walked with Zed and Tuesday, laughing and chatting the whole way, until they reached the palace's main entry hall. As they came down the final flight of stairs, Zed and Tuesday headed straight for the dining room, then stopped in confusion when they realized Bastian had made a left turn, heading for the stairwell to the kitchens.

"Where are you going?" Zed asked. "The dining room is this way."

For the first time, Bastian lost his breezy grin. "Oh. I guess I hadn't…" There was an awkward pause. "The staff dining hall is downstairs."

Tuesday's face burned with embarrassment. Her pulse pounded in her ears, which were also burning.

Lunches were usually delivered to wherever the day's activities brought her, but her family always ate breakfast and dinner together in a private dining room. True, it was far more modest than the palace's lavish banquet hall, which could seat hundreds of people—that one was reserved for special occasions, like the upcoming coronation feast—but there was no denying it felt like eating in a fancy restaurant twice a day, with porters delivering steaming platters of gourmet food. She never had to help set the table or wash the dishes, as she had for family dinners back home, or help the kitchen staff prepare the meal, as she had at the Resistance base. In fact, for the first time in her life, she was never assigned any chores at all.

Why had it never seemed strange that her family ate alone? Now that she thought about it, there were dozens of people working in the palace: cooks and cleaners, of course, but also mechanics, stable hands, and gardeners. Her mother had at least ten advisors, not to mention Gilford, the tailor and his apprentice, and all the guards… but she'd never really thought about what they did when they weren't working. For the first time, Tuesday realized all those people called the palace home, too. In fact, it might be more accurate to say that by moving into the palace, she was invading *their* home.

"Come eat with us!" Zed offered. "I'm sure my parents would like to meet you. And Baba—I mean, my grandmother is visiting this week, and—"

Bastian laughed nervously. "I appreciate the invitation, but I'm not sure that would go over so well. Staff meals are pretty casual. It's fun, though! There's a big buffet, so you can choose whatever you want to eat, and people from all different departments sit together at one long table, and—" He caught himself rambling, and laughed again. "Well, let's just say I'm not used to worrying about which fork to use, or afraid of breaking expensive dishes. An invitation to the Princess's table sounds a bit stressful."

Tuesday never asked for any kind of special treatment, and she didn't want Bastian to get the impression her family thought themselves too important to mix with the rest of the palace inhabitants. "Maybe we should have dinner with you, then," she suggested. "The staff meals sound like a lot more fun."

But Bastian shook his head. "No offense, but I'm not sure the others would be comfortable with visitors. I mean… you understand your family is in charge of everyone, right? And I don't just mean the Princess. Your dad's the Captain of the Guard, and your great-grandma supervises all the service jobs. Even your grandmother—didn't she used to be the Resistance General? When Tyrren got arrested, his butler and all his advisors quit, not to mention half the guards. I hear most of their replacements were hired out of the Resistance base, so your grandma used to be in charge of all of those people, too. Literally the entire palace reports to some member of your family. It's tough to relax while sitting next to your boss, you know?"

Tuesday tried to argue, but Bastian held up a hand and forced a smile. "I know, I know. But even if it's you, and not your parents, people would still worry about making a good impression. They'd wonder what gossip you might take home with you afterwards."

"Look, none of this was my idea," said Tuesday testily. "All I ever wanted was to move on with my life as a normal, average kid. We never fit in back home, what with Mom and Dad acting all weird and suspicious. I thought when we moved to Falinnheim we'd finally get to blend in. Zed and I don't want to be treated different from anyone else."

"I get it," Bastian assured her. "I really do. But like it or not, you *are* different. I mean, not to me. I don't have a job to get fired from anyway, and you and Zed seem fun. But to everyone else, you're royalty. You're like some expensive statue they have to be extra-careful not to bump into, because if they break it, there will be consequences. So if you want to be nice to the staff, the best way to do that is to give them space when they're off duty."

Tuesday tried to come up with a response, but all she could do was stand there, opening and closing her mouth in silent argument like a fish out of water. Which, coincidentally, described her dilemma perfectly.

"It's okay," said Zed quietly, giving her elbow a supportive squeeze. "No one thinks you're a spoiled brat, I promise. Now let's go. Everyone's waiting."

"See you tomorrow!" Bastian called, putting back on his carefree manner. "I want to hear more about this not-Falinnheim place you've been hanging out in. Sounds way more exciting than here, that's for sure!"

Tuesday sighed as she watched him disappear down the stairs. "Not really," she mumbled to herself. "Turns out things in Falinnheim are just the same."

———

Maisie's popovers looked as warm and buttery as ever, but for some reason Tuesday wasn't hungry anymore. She slouched over the polished table and nudged a neglected asparagus spear with her fork.

"How was your first lesson with Gilford?" her father asked between bites of his steamed mackerel.

"Fine," Tuesday moped in her best Not Fine voice.

"Care to elaborate?"

"Nope."

Zed decided to come to her rescue. He shared a few tidbits he remembered from the librarian's tour of the art collections, and about Bastian joining the class. (He decided not to bring up exactly *how* Bastian had made his dramatic entrance or mention the boy's side tour of his own even more exclusive collection.)

"It's a good thing you let Gilford know about the other Earth," Zed finished with a nod at his mother. "I always felt lost in Professor Orpin's class back at the base. He skipped right over all the Falinnheim basics he assumed we already knew. I get that we still need to keep some things a secret—at least from most people—but I'm glad we can actually ask Gilford questions without seeming suspicious. Or, you know… just stupid."

Princess Theadora looked up from her plate wearing a curious expression. For a moment she didn't speak, she just peered thoughtfully across the table at Zed. "How perceptive of him," she said at last.

Tuesday was still busy moping, but she couldn't miss the sudden calculating edge in her mother's voice. "What's that supposed to mean?"

Her mother paused, but then shook her head and let out a small laugh. "I must have forgotten, that's all. I've been so busy lately."

"Forgotten what?" Tuesday pressed.

"Never mind," she answered with a dismissive wave. "Of course Gilford needs to know what parts of your education he should catch up on. Royal Librarian is a trusted position; Gilford has been the librarian since I was a child, in fact. He'll have no trouble keeping classified information to himself. It's just—" She laughed again. "I can't seem to recall telling him about the other Earth."

Zed and Tuesday locked eyes across the table. Tuesday opened her mouth, but Zed cut her off before she could argue the point further. Something strange was going on, he was sure of it. But he was also sure they'd make better progress investigating whatever it was if the adults didn't start meddling. It was time to steer the conversation somewhere else. *Anywhere* else.

"Our next class isn't until tomorrow afternoon," he said, looking hopefully across the table at Baba, "so we have all morning free to do something fun. I was thinking maybe we could check out the palace grounds?"

"The head gardener is working on planting a hedge maze out behind the fountain courtyard," said Obaachan. "You should bring the children for a look," she added, turning to Baba.

Baba pulled a glass sphere out of her pocket and flicked her finger across the surface until it brought up the information she was looking for. "It's supposed to rain all morning tomorrow," she said with a frown.

"Don't be such a limp noodle!" Obaachan scolded. "A little water never hurt anyone. Wear a cloak. It'll be fine."

"Not if there's lightning," said Baba.

Zed wasn't about to let his grandmother off the hook so easily. This may have started as a distraction, but now that he'd set the words free, he realized he really *did* want to spend the morning with Baba. And besides, if he didn't come up with something to keep her busy, she'd be looking for ways to check in at work. "How about we look around the conservatory instead?" he suggested. "Should have a bunch of rare plant samples."

Tuesday let out a longsuffering sigh. Touring a room full of plants you couldn't even eat sounded suspiciously like something Gilford would suggest. Leave it to her brother to kiss up to the teacher when he wasn't even here. But then she remembered something she'd overheard Baba say back at the base, which made her realize what Zed was up to.

"Didn't you say you used to be a florist?" Tuesday asked.

Baba looked up in surprise. "Yes, I was. That was a long

time ago, though. How did you know that?"

"I pay attention," said Tuesday. "Anyway, I bet the conservatory has tons of flowers. Weird ones you wouldn't usually get to see. Could be fun, I guess."

"Go on, Mom," Tuesday's father urged. "You'll love it."

Maybe it was her son's encouragement that finally melted Baba's hesitance. Or maybe she just ran out of excuses to refuse, since the conservatory was indoors. Either way, her doubtful expression was finally replaced by a rare smile. "That sounds great," she agreed.

"Let's just hope we don't bump into Professor Plum or Colonel Mustard," Zed added brightly.

Tuesday tilted her head and stared at him like he'd just suggested they take up Jello juggling. Everyone else looked equally befuddled.

"You know…" he prodded, "like the game? Colonel Mustard, with the candlestick, in the conservatory?"

Tuesday rolled her eyes so hard she nearly caught a glimpse of her own brain. The adults were still exchanging puzzled glances. Tuesday hadn't expected Baba and Obaachan to get it, but it seemed even Mom and Dad were left in the dark this time. Apparently their study of the other Earth hadn't covered board games.

She wasn't about to reward such a poor attempt at a joke by actually *laughing*—if Zed got on a roll with that kind of thing, he'd be tossing out puns left and right—but it did get her thinking. Luckily there wasn't a murder to investigate, but she had to admit her new life had some shocking similarities to a mystery-solving game. She lived in a huge old house with its own conservatory, a private library, and at least a few secret passages. Maybe…

Yes.

Tuesday made her decision. It was time to use Falinnheim's weirdness to her advantage for a change. Time to play a little game of her own.

CHAPTER 5
IN THE CONSERVATORY

Just as Baba's crystal ball had predicted, Tuesday was awakened the next morning by the steady drumbeat of raindrops splattering her bedroom windows. The forecast was wrong about the lightning, but that hardly mattered. Even without the threat of electrocution, she had no intention of going outside today. Cloak or not, she'd have been drenched in seconds.

She dressed hastily (which was unfortunate, as she later discovered she'd chosen mismatched socks) and raced through breakfast (which was slightly more fortunate, as it meant she finished her toast and scrambled eggs before Nyx had time to "borrow" any from her plate.) She didn't really care about rare plants, but checking out the conservatory's collection had to be a better use of her morning than listening to whatever topic Gilford wanted to drone on about. And besides, if she beat Zed and Baba there, she might have a chance to look for more secret passages.

Like the rest of the palace's windows, the conservatory's glass dome showed nothing but slate-gray skies and persistent raindrops. But unlike in the rest of the palace (which, despite being decorated with endless tapestries and rugs, always felt rather cold and clammy), Tuesday was surprised to find the conservatory pleasantly warm. Not oppressively so, like the greenhouse back at the base— weeding duty in the greenhouse had always felt like going for a swim in a steaming bowl of chowder. The conservatory reminded Tuesday of a perfect, sunny afternoon in late June, as opposed to what today actually was: a morning downpour barely a week into March. (Or at least that's what the calendar back home would have called it.)

Tuesday scanned the winding paths, paved with black pebbles, and the masses of colorful leaves sprouting beside them. There was only one obvious doorway connecting the conservatory with the rest of the palace, but that didn't mean anything. After all, the whole point of a secret passage is for the door to be as un-obvious as possible. Also, it didn't have to connect with the palace. This would be the perfect place to hide a tunnel to the grounds…

She chose a raised planting bed and parted leaves the size of elephants' ears, searching for anything that looked out of place. When nothing caught her eye, she leaned in a little further, and then further still, until at last she found herself kneeling on the flagstone border with her entire upper half swallowed by a massive flowering shrub.

"Digging for buried treasure?"

"AAUGH!" Though Tuesday knew she wasn't doing anything to feel guilty about, suddenly discovering she wasn't alone caught her so off guard that she panicked and fell the rest of the way into the bush. When she managed to scramble back out of it, knees now blackened with mulch stains and her hair a tangle of twigs, she was met by Bastian's mischievous smile.

"Good morning, Your Highness."

Thankfully he ignored her disheveled state, but that didn't stop her ears from burning. "Don't call me that," Tuesday huffed, picking leaves out of her hair. "And what are *you* doing here?"

Bastian grinned even wider. "I might ask you the same thing."

Tuesday answered him with a scowl.

"I came to check on Liz," he said. "Want to help me look for her?"

"Who's Liz?"

Before Bastian could explain, Nyx came barreling down the path toward them. After collecting a resigned sigh from Tuesday and some ear scritches from Bastian, she was off again, loping along the walkways until something caught her attention, snuffling for a moment in the foliage, then dashing along again to find more novelties to sniff.

"Hey Tuesday, wait up!" Zed strolled around a bank of tall decorative grasses to join them but stopped short when he caught sight of his sister. "What happened to you?" he asked, looking her skeptically up and down. "Did you lose a fight or something?"

"I tripped," said Tuesday hotly.

"Into the compost bin?"

"Never mind!" she shot back, glaring at Bastian as he joined Zed in laughing. "This is no time for jokes. We've got to find Liz."

"Who?" Zed asked.

But Bastian's explanation was delayed again, this time by Nyx, who let out a yelp from somewhere out of sight. At least Tuesday assumed it must have been the dog—who else could it be?—but she couldn't remember ever hearing her pet make that sound before. If Nyx was startled or injured, she was more likely to go into Flaming Attack Mode than ask for help.

Everyone followed the noise to the far corner of the conservatory, where they found Nyx standing in the middle of the footpath, her head tilted quizzically. She was no longer yelping, and she didn't seem hurt. Just... deeply confused.

Zed paused, tilting his head to match. "What's that hanging off her chin?"

"It looks like some sort of lizard," said Tuesday.

"Liz!" Bastian ran up and scooped a hand under the tiny green lizard clamped onto Nyx's bottom lip. When the dangling reptile didn't let go, Bastian plucked a leaf the size of a dinner plate from the nearest plant bed and placed that under its feet instead. Finally the lizard released its hold on Nyx's lip, plopped onto the leaf, then squiggled its way up the sleeve of Bastian's tunic until only the tip of its long, thin tail was left exposed.

"Well, looks like we found Liz," said Zed.

"Real original name for a lizard," Tuesday scoffed.

"Oh, that's just for short," said Bastian, lightly stroking Liz's tail with a fingertip. "Her full name is Queen Elizardabeth."

Tuesday groaned. Zed burst into a fresh round of giggles. Nyx shook herself off and trotted away to find more plants to stick her nose into.

"What's so funny?" called a familiar voice.

Everyone turned to see who it was. When Bastian caught sight of Princess Theadora strolling along the path, he hastily arranged himself into a stiff bow.

"Knock that off," Tuesday muttered to him. "It's only Mom."

"Easy for you to say," Bastian whispered back.

Zed stepped in to explain that Nyx had had a small disagreement with an even smaller lizard, and Bastian assured the Princess that her pet had not been injured. "Queen Elizardabeth doesn't even have teeth," he said. "She just got a bit nervous, being sniffed by a giant nose all of the sudden. Not that Nyx's nose is *too* big, or anything. It's just the right size for a Gabriel Hound! At least, I imagine it is… I've never really seen another Gabriel Houn—"

But Bastian's rambling was soon buried by the Princess's laughter. "What a clever name! Where did you come up with it?"

"Oh, it just reminded me of a story Uncle Gilford used to tell when I was little. He said there was a queen long ago who was Shakespeare's biggest fan, so Shakespeare had to write compliments to her into his plays." He laughed. "Queen Elizabeth sounds just as feisty as a lizard who bites first and asks questions later."

Tuesday's shock fell out of her mouth before she could stop it. "You know about Shakespeare?"

Her mother raised an eyebrow at her. "Do you… *not* know Shakespeare? I'll have to let Gilford know you need a refresher course on classic literature."

"Of course *I've* heard of him, but how—"

"He's one of Falinnheim's most celebrated writers," the Princess went on. "Why, half the English language would be different without his influence."

Tuesday opened her mouth, but Zed silenced her with a look before any more arguments could spill out. Time to change the subject before Mom started asking questions of her own. "What brings you to the conservatory?" he asked (a bit too cheerfully.) "I thought you had a busy day lined up."

"I do, in fact—very busy. Nyx seemed alarmed for a moment, so I thought there might be some kind of problem. But it sounds like everything's fine after all."

Tuesday groaned, but she tried to keep it to herself. Of course! Mom and Nyx could read each other's minds. Or… something. She wasn't totally sure how their connection worked, but one thing was certain: getting any secret investigating done was going to be a lot tougher with Mom's furry spy watching her every move.

"We're just fine here, Your Majesty," said Bastian with another bow. "Thank you for your concern. Enjoy your meetings."

Princess Theadora smiled, but the laugh that followed was anything but amused. She acted like Bastian had just wished her a happy root canal. "I appreciate the sentiment," she said grimly, "but I definitely won't be enjoying this one."

"Why?" asked Tuesday. "What are your advisors talking about today?

The Princess sighed. "We have to figure out what to do with Tyrren."

The three kids waited in confused silence as the Princess excused herself and left the conservatory. Only when they were alone again did Zed say what they were all thinking: "What's that supposed to mean?"

"Beats me," said Tuesday. "Tyrren's trial ended weeks ago. Obaachan said it was an easy conviction—they had all kinds of witnesses and evidence and everything. Seems pretty dealt with to me."

This was true. Zed and Tuesday hadn't been called on to

testify at Tyrren's trial—in fact, their parents had forbidden them from being involved in any way, even as spectators—but in the end, it didn't matter. People had lined up from all over Falinnheim to present evidence of the former dictator's crimes. The spies of the Red Hand had gone into hiding the moment Tyrren was arrested, but the investigators had managed to locate all the former palace guards who had carried out Tyrren's initial attack. And since the guards had promptly blamed each other, their trials had concluded without much fuss, either. Sure, there was still the matter of rounding up the last few fugitives, but it was only a matter of time—after all, with Scrimbley's compass broken, it was impossible to leave Falinnheim, so the Red Hand couldn't hide out forever. With Tyrren in jail, there didn't seem to be much else to worry about. But then, Tuesday decided privately, Mom had been doing nothing *but* worrying, lately. Maybe she just couldn't help herself.

Baba made her entrance to the conservatory just as the Princess strode out. Bastian managed to keep his cool this time, since he wasn't required to bow to a retired rebel. The four of them spent a relaxing morning wandering the winding paths, listening to the raindrops pattering overhead while Baba pointed out interesting plant samples like the Night Lily or Button Cactus. Tuesday didn't locate any secret tunnels, but she made a mental note of some likely locations to come back and investigate next time she got a moment alone. Nyx and Queen Elizardabeth managed to avoid any more unpleasant confrontations. But though Zed's feet spent the morning on a leisurely stroll, his mind raced in circles like it was stuck on a hamster wheel. He silently rehearsed the evidence, determined not to forget a single detail before he had a chance to plot the points in his notebook:

—OKAY, SO—

- Scrimbley said Falinnheim hasn't been in contact with the rest of Earth for 400 years
- No one here recognizes nursery rhymes or board games (chess doesn't count—it's super old)
- Calendars and holidays are different
- Baba, Captain Solomon, and Bastian didn't know about the other Earth until we told them
- Gilford already knew (somehow???) but he says we still have to keep the other Earth a secret

—BUT—

- Where would Bastian's great-grandma get a bunch of Other Earth stuff from 1918?
- Pretty sure Queen Elizabeth ruled England, not Falinnheim
- How does Bastian know about Shakespeare? He didn't write any of the books in the bunker
- Mom has lived both places—did she forget which world Shakespeare was from?
- Would Mom really forget telling Gilford why we needed to catch up on Falinnheim's history?

No doubt about it, something weird was going on. He and Tuesday no longer had a treehouse, but they'd have to make do without it.

It was time to call a meeting.

CHAPTER 6
THE PRIME SUSPECT

It was potato soup for lunch today—Zed's favorite. Normally he would have tried to sweet-talk Baba into a chess rematch while they ate, counting on her intimidating Gilford into bending that pesky "no food in the library" rule. But today was anything but normal. The morning's garden tour got cut short when a messenger marched into the conservatory and made his announcement: Princess Theadora officially requested the former general's counsel in a classified meeting. Baba sighed and made her apologies, but this time, Zed wasn't all that disappointed about the interruption. "Don't worry, Baba," he'd said, shooting his grandmother his most persuasive smile. "We'll find a way to keep busy."

At Zed's insistence, the kids collected their lunch trays from the kitchen themselves, before any of the serving staff could come looking for them, and retreated to the bunker to talk things over alone.

"I still don't see what all the fuss is about," Bastian mumbled through a mouthful of soup. He pointed at the evidence list Zed had copied down from his notebook and tacked up on the crate shelves. "Uncle Gil's been gushing about how great Shakespeare is since before I was even old enough to read, let alone understand all the old-timey language. Why is it suspicious the Princess has heard of him too?"

"None of you should know Shakespeare!" Zed insisted. "He's not from Falinnheim at all—he's from the other Earth."

"But he died four hundred years ago," Bastian pointed out. "It's not like anyone alive has met him. How do you know he wasn't from Falinnheim all along? Maybe it's the other Earth that borrowed his stories."

"Four hundred years..." Tuesday repeated. She scrambled up from her floor cushion for a better look at Zed's list. "That's exactly how long Scrimbley said the transporter compasses have been banned."

"So if transporting between worlds was still legal while Shakespeare was alive," Zed reasoned, "that means written copies of his work could have been carried back and forth."

"Or—who knows?" Bastian added, "maybe he was a traveler himself."

Zed was trying to keep an open mind about the whole thing—if the timeline worked out, technically it was possible—but the evidence didn't seem to be in Bastian's favor. "What about all the places Shakespeare wrote about?

Like… doesn't *Macbeth* take place in Scotland? And I'm pretty sure there's a play called *The Merchant of Venice*. Those are definitely from the other Earth. Why would he write about places the audience wouldn't know?"

"Not to mention London," Tuesday added. "Shakespeare had a theater there, I'm pretty sure."

For some odd reason, Bastian started laughing. "Now you're just messing with me," he said, wagging an accusing finger at Tuesday. "London's imaginary!"

Tuesday stared at him, perplexed. "No?"

"Oh come on," Bastian insisted, "London's in a bunch of stories. Peter Pan and Sherlock Holmes both talk about London, and they aren't real either, you know."

"Wait, now you know Sherlock Holmes, too? He wasn't in any of the books you showed us."

"That's because he's not from a book," Bastian said with a shrug. "Here, see for yourself." He scooted over to the jumble of papers on the crate shelves and pulled out a dog-eared magazine. He flipped past several black and white illustrations until he found the page he wanted, then handed it to Tuesday.

"The Valley of Fear," she read aloud, "a new Sherlock Holmes story by A. Conan Doyle." Her eyes flicked to the page heading. "*The Strand* magazine. January, 1915."

"See?" said Bastian smugly. "London's just a place from stories. Like Oz, or Neverland." He laughed again. "I mean, it's not like there's really a land called India full of talking animals, just because *The Jungle Book* says so."

Zed tried to break the news to Bastian without making him feel stupid. "Look, we know the stories are made up, but those are all real places. Well, not *all* of them—Neverland and Oz are imaginary—but India and London are real."

"Have you ever been there?" Bastian argued.

"Well, no," Zed was forced to admit. "But I've seen them on maps."

Bastian just rolled his eyes. "Stop trying to prank me. Next you'll be saying there *really are* giant wind storms in a place called Kansas."

"There are!" Tuesday protested.

Nyx chose this moment to sample the rest of Tuesday's soup, which provided just enough distraction to dislodge the stalemate.

"Let's go over what we know for sure," Zed suggested. "There are two worlds that mostly don't know about each other. There are ways to travel between them. Travel from Falinnheim to the other Earth has been illegal for hundreds of years, but we have evidence that a few people have been doing it anyway."

"Okay," Bastian conceded. "Let's say, just for argument's sake, that you're right. What's any of it got to do with us?"

Tuesday threw her hands up in exasperation. "Aren't you the least bit curious? People don't work this hard to keep secrets unless they know something *important.* I'm getting pretty sick of all the adults refusing to tell us anything!”

“Tell that to Uncle Gil,” Bastian scoffed. “He never *stops* trying to talk my ear off.”

“Gilford!” Zed repeated. “That’s it!”

Bastian and Tuesday stared at him.

“Don’t you see? Gilford is the one person connecting all the evidence. He told *you* about Shakespeare and Queen Elizabeth,” Zed explained, pointing at Bastian, “which he shouldn’t know. And he told *me* that Mom talked to him about the other Earth, which she can’t remember doing. He’d need a pretty good reason to risk lying about it.”

“Remember what Mom said about Gilford?” Tuesday added. “She admitted she couldn’t remember telling him about the other Earth, but she wasn’t worried, because she ought to be able to trust the Royal Librarian with a secret. She said Gilford has had the job since she was a kid.”

“Right…” said Zed. “Where are you going with this?”

“Gilford told us himself that the Royal Librarian is also the palace tutor. In the palace where Mom grew up. So that means…”

“Gilford was Mom’s teacher too,” Zed finished for her.

“I guess that might explain where she heard about Shakespeare,” said Bastian. “Uncle Gil can’t resist gabbing on about books. He probably wasn’t any different thirty years ago.”

“So if he’s usually such a blabbermouth, why would Gilford start keeping secrets now?” Zed wondered.

A realization tiptoed into Tuesday's mind. "The only reason you got the books from your great-grandma's trunk was because Gilford didn't want them," she told Bastian. "What if the trunk had other stuff in it too—things he *did* keep? It would have to be a really amazing discovery to convince him to keep his mouth shut, don't you think?"

"I guess it's possible," said Bastian. "But how would we know? We can't just walk up and ask him. If he found something worth keeping secret, he's not likely to admit it now."

"Plus that would totally tip him off we're investigating," Tuesday agreed. "Whatever he might have kept from the trunk, we're better off searching for it ourselves."

"Okay, think," said Zed. "Where would Gilford hide something important?"

But they didn't really have to think about it—they knew exactly where Gilford kept the things he cared about.

The three kids nodded in unison. "The library."

CHAPTER 7
THE SECRETS OF
THE ROYAL LIBRARY

The plan was simple: all they had to do was distract Gilford long enough to take a quick snoop through his desk. And when it came to convenient distractions, they knew exactly who to turn to. It didn't even matter what Nyx did—her very presence was enough to make Gilford flustered. Hopefully, flustered enough to overlook a missing student or two.

They made their way to the library twenty minutes early, hoping to beat Gilford back from his lunch break, but no such luck—there he was, crouched over his desk, examining an unfurled scroll of parchment with a magnifying glass. Right on cue, Nyx flumped herself down between the chess table and the dictionary stand and started digging at one ear with a back paw.

"That beast better not have fleas," Gilford said without

looking up. "I have enough trouble keeping the paper mites at bay without inviting more pests into the library."

"Nonsense," Bastian argued, "fleas don't eat paper."

Tuesday kicked him in the leg.

"I mean," he backtracked, catching the hint, "*do* fleas eat paper? That would be just terrible for the books. But how can we know?"

Tuesday slapped on her most innocent, doe-eyed expression. "This sounds serious. We'd better make sure. Gilford, could you show us how to look up the answer?"

Just as Tuesday had hoped, Gilford couldn't resist students actually showing an interest in learning. "First," he said, standing up and smoothing his goatee, "we need to head for the nonfiction section, which is over in the southeast quadrant. From there we can check the directory for—"

Gilford's voice faded as he led Bastian, Tuesday, and Nyx through the forest of bookshelves. As soon as they were out of sight, Zed slunk to Gilford's desk and quietly eased open its various cabinets and drawers. He found a fountain pen and a dozen discarded nibs, a book of nature poetry, a blank notebook, and a half-eaten bean sprout sandwich—so much for that "no food in the library" rule—but nothing that seemed particularly suspicious. He even felt along the bottoms and backs of all the drawers, checking for false panels or hidden compartments, but came up empty. Finally Zed put his back to the floor and slid under the desk to check for buttons or switches that might unlock hidden secrets.

"—and so you see, based on Professor Ogumbe's research into various branches of the arthropod phylum, the taxonomy of the so-called paper mite—actually a type of louse—means it's more closely related to the common flea than it is to true mites, which are technically arachnids." Gilford had returned with a book, Tuesday and Bastian in tow, and was heading for his desk! Zed tucked in his legs so he was completely hidden underneath it. He waited for Gilford to take his seat behind the desk, then slithered out the opposite side and crouched in front of it. Gilford was so busy explaining the bug chart he'd found that he didn't even notice Zed stand up on the other side of the desk and lean in for a closer look at the book. It was like he'd been with them the entire time.

Tuesday stood behind Gilford so she could motion to Zed without being seen. "Anything?" she mouthed silently at him.

Zed shook his head.

Tuesday wasn't ready to give up yet. Just because Gilford's desk came up clean didn't mean he had nothing to hide. He could have stashed the evidence anywhere. In fact, with endless rows of books, scrolls, and historic collections at his fingertips, the librarian could even hide things in plain sight...

"I'll be right back," Tuesday announced suddenly. "I think I dropped my..." She mumbled the end of the sentence, not even bothering to come up with a decent excuse to disappear into the rows of shelves.

She'd already browsed the nonfiction section; Tuesday had followed Gilford as slowly as possible on his trip to retrieve the bug chart, scanning every row they passed for anything that seemed out of place. She decided to give fiction a try.

"Find anything?"

Tuesday jumped. But it was only Zed, who had snuck up behind her to join the search.

"We can't *all* go missing!" Tuesday hissed at him. "I don't care how much Gilford likes hearing himself talk. If no one's left to listen, he's bound to notice eventually."

"Relax," Zed whispered back, "he's on a flea hunt. Bastian's got him searching through Nyx's coat with a magnifying glass."

"Meanwhile, we're on a wild goose chase," Tuesday grumbled. "I don't even know where to start! There's so many books, and we're not sure what we're looking for."

"How about Shakespeare?" Zed suggested.

Based on Bastian's evidence, it sounded like Gilford must have known about Shakespeare long before the mysterious trunk was discovered. Still, it was as good a place to start as any. And since fiction was shelved alphabetically by author, they wouldn't even have to search the directory to find him.

They followed the lettered shelves until they found the one marked S tucked into the library's southwest corner. Zed ran his fingers along the books' spines, inspecting the names until he found Shakespeare. The playwright had an entire shelf to himself, from *A Midsummer Night's Dream* to *Twelfth Night*. Zed was familiar with *Romeo and Juliet* and *Hamlet*, but most of the other titles were new to him. He pulled a copy of *Antony and Cleopatra* off the shelf and flipped through the pages.

"Okay…" Tuesday whispered. "We found Shakespeare. Now what?"

Zed shrugged. "It's weird that his books are here at all, but that doesn't really tell us much."

Tuesday rolled her eyes. Looking up Shakespeare had been Zed's idea in the first place, but whatever. She started pulling the books off the shelf one by one and flipping through them, hoping there might be a secret envelope tucked between the pages, or instructions written on the shelf behind the books, or… something.

All the books seemed depressingly ordinary. At least, they were until she got to the middle of the row. Tuesday slid *King Lear* back into place, then reached for the next book.

The book refused to budge.

"Bingo!" Tuesday braced one foot against the shelf and tugged with both hands, but the book was thoroughly stuck. She decided to remove all the other books from the shelf so she could get a better look at whatever mechanism was holding it in place.

"*Love's Labour's Lost*," said Zed, peering over Tuesday's shoulder to read the title. "Also by William Shakespeare. I wonder what's so special about this one?"

"We'll never know if we can't pick it up." Tuesday stretched on her tiptoes for a better look. She couldn't find any sort of latch or hinge around the book's edges. What was locking it down?

"Maybe it's glued to the shelf," Zed suggested. He tried lifting the book straight up, instead of sliding it. He tried tipping it to each side. But nothing worked.

"What would be the point of that?" Tuesday argued.

"The point of what?" said a voice behind them.

Zed and Tuesday both jumped this time. Bastian had joined the search party.

"You're supposed to be keeping Gilford distracted!" said Tuesday.

"He sent me to look for you two. He's still busy flea hunting, but he hasn't found a single one and he's losing focus. We'd better hurry up."

"Easy for you to say," Tuesday grumbled. "*You* figure out how to move the book, if you're so smart."

"What are you talking about? Just pick it up."

And to Tuesday and Zed's astonishment, Bastian did exactly that.

"How did you—?" Tuesday started, but there was no time to talk. Bastian didn't even have time to open the book. The moment it left the shelf the entire bookcase swung inward like a door. Where the wall behind it should have been, instead they found a small, dark closet.

"*Now* we're getting somewhere!" Bastian cheered. He tucked *Love's Labour's Lost* under his arm and darted inside, pulling Zed and Tuesday with him.

Like all the other hidden spaces in the palace, the library closet had rows of crystals built into the walls, which lit up when the bookshelf door closed behind them. Inside they found more bookshelves, stacked floor to ceiling with yellowed scrolls of parchment, dusty leather-bound books, and even sheets of stamped metal and engraved stone, each one covered in writing.

"Whoa," said Zed, turning on the spot to take it all in. "There's no way all this would have fit in your great-grandma's trunk."

"Uncle Gil can't have collected all of this himself," said Bastian. "The Royal Librarians must have been working on this since... well, ever since there were librarians, I guess."

"Why hide this stuff in a closet?" Tuesday wondered aloud. "Gilford said all the previous rulers' artifacts are locked in the palace vault. If these books are so special, why not keep them there, instead?"

"We can figure that out later," said Zed. "We've gotta get the Shakespeare shelf put back together before Gilford comes looking for us."

Opening the closet in the first place was a huge achievement, but since Tuesday wasn't sure how Bastian had managed it, she couldn't count on being able to get in here again. She wasn't about to leave without something to show for it. There was just one problem: as she scanned the shelves in search of the perfect book to smuggle out with her, she realized she couldn't read any of them. "They're all in different languages!"

Some books used the alphabet Tuesday was used to, but with the letters jumbled up in an unfamiliar order. Others were covered in characters she'd never seen before. A couple of the scrolls featured what looked like ancient Egyptian hieroglyphs. And then there were records that weren't even made of paper: stone tiles, stamped sheets of copper, and even something that appeared to be a shard of bone, all engraved with pictures and symbols.

"Not all of them." Zed pointed to a dark blue volume on the highest shelf. "This one's in English."

"*The Book of the Founders,*" Tuesday read aloud, squinting up at the title. Below the spine's silver lettering, she could just make out a tiny emblem that looked like some kind of bird. No—it was two birds. They were perched so close together it was hard to tell their bodies apart, but their beaks faced in opposite directions. One looking forward, one looking back. The art style was different, but she knew exactly where she'd seen that symbol before: it was on the royal crest embedded in her mother's slipsteel ring.

Tuesday started climbing the shelves to retrieve the book, but Bastian was tall enough to reach up and grab it before she'd even found a decent foothold. He passed the book off to Zed and ushered everyone back out of the hidden room.

They couldn't just walk around with a contraband book all day. If Gilford caught sight of it, he'd take an immediate interest in their reading selection. And it was far too thick to hide inside the cover of a different book. So while Tuesday and Bastian rushed to return all the Shakespeare volumes to their places, Zed searched for a place to stash their find.

If the "hide in plain sight" strategy had worked for shelving Shakespeare, Zed figured, why not try the same thing himself? He walked two rows over, back to the center of the library, and found the row of fiction marked F. He slid *The Book of the Founders* into the place it would sit alphabetically if the word Founders had been the author. That should be easy enough to find again, when the day's lessons were over. Then they could ferry it out of the library with the rest of their school books, and Gilford would be none the wiser.

Zed made it back to the S section just as Bastian put the last book in place. The moment *Love's Labour's Lost* touched the shelf the bookcase door closed itself automatically, then locked in place with a *click*.

"It's almost like a key," Tuesday muttered. "Except you open the door by removing the key, instead of inserting it." She tried once more to pick the Shakespeare volume up, but it still refused to budge.

"We can figure that part out later," Bastian reminded her. "Right now, we need to get as far from here as possible." He did a stealthy speedwalk along the aisles and motioned for Zed and Tuesday to follow him.

"Good thinking," Zed whispered. "It would look really suspicious to be standing in front of a secret door we shouldn't know about when—"

"*There* you three are!" Gilford had arrived, Nyx at his heels, and he looked as irritated as a poison ivy rash. "What in Zeus's name could have taken you this long?"

"I'm sorry, Gilford," Tuesday fumbled, "I was just looking for my lost, uh…"

"Keys!" said Bastian, at the exact same moment Zed blurted out, "Bookmark!"

"My favorite bookmark, with a *picture* of keys on it," Tuesday added. "Because reading is the key to knowledge, you know?"

Gilford raised an eyebrow at them, but apparently he was too anxious to get the class back on track to think too hard about the odd exchange. "I'll be sure to keep an eye out for it," he said. "Now please, back to the study tables. We really must get on with our geography lesson."

Bastian offered Nyx a quick chin scritch, then followed along as Gilford turned on his heel and marched to the front of the library.

Tuesday and Zed joined the procession, but not before exchanging a silent fist bump behind Gilford's back.

———————

The rain stopped, the clouds parted, and the first rays of a brilliant orange sunset were streaming through the library's arched windows by the time Gilford finally lost steam. They'd spent hours poring over maps, comparing ancient hand-drawn depictions of Falinnheim's borders to the modern digital versions available on electronic tablets. But the lesson didn't really break up until the messenger arrived.

"The Regent sends her apologies," the man said, bowing stiffly at Tuesday and Zed. "Today's meeting has gone on longer than expected, and Captain Beren and the Chief of Staff have been asked to contribute to the negotiations as well."

"He means Dad and Obaachan," Tuesday told Zed.

"I know that!" Zed huffed.

"As such," the messenger continued, "they will not be available to join you for dinner. Her Majesty asks that you take your meals privately this evening."

Normally Zed would have been disappointed—if this morning's meeting was still going on, that meant Baba was stuck in there too—but the way this day was going, he'd already abandoned any hope of normality. And for once, all the adults being too busy to pay attention to him was exactly what he'd hoped for. His eyes darted over to the library shelves.

"No problem," said Gilford. "We'll take a quick dinner break, then meet back here for an evening study session."

Tuesday and Bastian exchanged horrified looks, but the messenger spoke up before anyone could protest. "I'm afraid not," he said, bowing to Gilford this time. "Her

Majesty has requested the Royal Librarian's counsel in the meeting as well. You are to report to the conference chambers immediately."

Gilford's face lit up like the messenger had just offered him a sack of gold-plated rainbows. It took him a second to put his Serious Business expression back on. "Of course," he said sternly, standing and straightening his shirt collar. "I would be honored to give the Regent my assistance."

He was halfway to the door before he remembered his students. He paused, then looked back over his shoulder at the three kids grinning a little too brightly at each other across the map-strewn table. "Are you sure you'll be all right without me? I suppose I could try to find a footman or something to keep an eye on you until the meeting ends… but this sounds like an important discussion, so it might take hours to resolve."

"Don't you worry, Uncle Gil," said Bastian with a wink. "We have plenty to do. This would be a perfect opportunity to catch up on some reading."

CHAPTER 8
THE BOOK OF THE FOUNDERS

Tuesday, Zed, and Bastian held their breaths as Gilford and the messenger strode out of the library. There was a moment of tense silence, and then two. When at last the echoing footsteps left the hall and they were sure Gilford wouldn't duck back in to leave them homework, everyone erupted in relieved laughter and traded high fives. After so many close calls finding the book in the first place, it looked like luck was finally on their side.

Tuesday accompanied Bastian to the kitchens, where he loaded a big metal tray with enough food to share. He asked the chef's apprentice to let his parents know he'd be back late. "School project," he explained. "Looks like it's gonna be a long one. You know how Uncle Gil is." By the time they made it back to the bunker, Zed and Nyx were already there waiting for them.

"All right," said Zed, settling in on the bank of floor cushions he'd arranged against one wall and opening the stolen book. "Time to get some answers!"

Bastian led Nyx to the opposite wall and set down the platter of roast trimmings, bread heels, and marrow bones the kitchen staff had collected for her. "That ought to keep you busy long enough to let us eat our own dinners in peace," he told the dog.

"Don't count on it," Tuesday warned.

"I can read out loud while you guys eat," Zed offered. "Then we'll trade off. Should be enough to keep Nyx from snatching all the food."

Bastian and Tuesday sat on either side of him, balancing their plates in their laps, and leaned over to get a better look at the title page. THE BOOK OF THE FOUNDERS, it read. A HISTORY OF THE PEOPLE AND EVENTS THAT SHAPED FALINNHEIM. TRANSLATED AND COMPILED BY THE ROYAL ARCHIVISTS.

Zed cleared his throat, turned the page, and began to read. "Chapter one," he said. "The Tale of Olav the Waymaster."

———

THE TALE OF OLAV THE WAYMASTER

It began long before Olav was a Waymaster. He wasn't even a Wayapprentice. Then, he was just regular Olav Orvaldsen.

Olav was not strong or handsome. He wasn't athletic,

or artistic, or even particularly clever. He always flubbed the punchlines of jokes and he never remembered anyone's birthday until three days after the fact. If you really must know, his cooking was nearly as dreadful as his fashion sense, his gurgling laugh made dogs howl and babies cry, and his singing voice was often compared to a bunch of rusty nails swirling around in a bucket of dirty mop water. Thankfully, Olav did have one advantage in life: he was short.

This might not seem like an advantage, but Olav thanked the stars every night for the blessing of his reduced stature. For although this meant he was even more distant from those stars than everyone else in the village of Björnvald, it also meant that he was not fit to be a viking, which suited Olav just fine. He had no interest in raiding, pillaging, or looting. In fact, he'd come dead last in Plundery at school, and when the children gathered on the village green for a game of Monks and Robbers, he was always the last one chosen for a team. Olav wasn't really sure what he wanted to do with his life, but as long as he was doing it on dry land, anything at all seemed fine to him.

As Olav grew up, he was relieved to notice his classmates kept growing right on past him. Every Friday he made a special trip down to the shipbuilder's yard to ensure he could still walk clear under the sign that read YOU MUST BE THIS TALL TO RAID. He made sure to comb his hair as flat as possible before measuring, just in case an unruly orange tuft might add enough height to put him over the edge. (This also meant he was the only lad in Björnvald who combed his hair with any regularity, which made his mother happy.) By the time his twenty-second birthday arrived, he was satisfied no proper viking would ever want him on their crew.

Unfortunately for Olav, there were no proper vikings in Björnvald. These scoundrels were as improper as they come. And though they knew Olav was as useless with a sword as he was with a stewpot, every viking crew needs someone to mend socks and scrub out latrine buckets. So that night they kidnapped Olav from his own birthday party, stuffed him in their ship's hold, and sailed off.

The vikings let him out of the dark, cramped hold the next morning, but being up on deck wasn't any better. For one thing, the deck was where the vikings spent all their time, and Olav wasn't eager to get any closer to them than absolutely necessary. Between their constant bickering and pungent body odor, it was enough to turn anyone's stomach. (Or perhaps it was the rocking motion of the ship? Whatever the reason, his stomach definitely wasn't on board with this voyage, which is why his lunch refused to stay on board either.)

After three days of battling seasickness and smelly socks, Olav was relieved to notice the return of the birds—first the seagulls, who mobbed the vikings' meals in hopes of snatching a discarded fish head or crumbling wayfarer's biscuit, and then the ravens, who bullied these spoils away from the seagulls—because this meant they were nearing land. And besides, ravens were known to be good luck. Legend said that the mighty god Odin kept a pair of raven messengers as pets, and Olav liked the idea that the ravens' next stop might be in Asgard to keep the All-Father updated on the ship's progress. At least then someone would be looking out for him. Olav didn't care if that seemed silly, to hope that these particular ravens might be telling Odin of his troubles. He needed all the help he could get.

Sure enough, as the sun slipped below the horizon that evening, the last rays of daylight fell on the jagged cliffs of a distant island. The vikings rowed through the night, and in the fourth watch their ship reached the island's rocky shore. The vikings had never pillaged this particular island before, but they were excited about its prospects because the large building at the top of the cliff looked a lot like a monastery. They *loved* pillaging monasteries.

Captain Sigrid explained to Olav that monasteries were full of monks. This was helpful for two reasons: first, in addition to praying and doodling silly illustrations in the margins of ancient manuscripts and whatever else monks did with their time, they typically took up some type of industry to support the monastery. Each monastery had a different specialty, but it didn't really matter what it was—whether they brewed ale or tended honeybees or baked cakes, the results were always delightfully stealable.

The second advantage to raiding monasteries was that all monks took religious vows, typically including vows of nonviolence, which conveniently prevented the monks from fighting back when the vikings made off with all their ale or honey or cakes. Even better, sometimes the monks hadn't yet spent the gold they'd earned from selling last month's goods, which meant it was hanging around the monastery waiting for the vikings to steal that, too.

"But I don't want to steal from monks!" Olav protested. He didn't really want to steal from anyone, but stealing from monks who couldn't even fight back seemed especially underhanded.

The captain laughed. "Who said you'd be coming along?" she sneered. "You'd bungle the attack anyway. You're going to stay here and protect the ship."

"Protect it from what?" Olav asked. But all the vikings ignored him and slunk off into the darkness to find a path up the cliff.

So, Olav waited with the ship. He had to wait a long time, and he got very bored. He wondered what was going on at the top of the cliff. Were the vikings taking a break to sample the monks' cakes before hauling the rest back to the ship? Or perhaps the search for stashed gold coins was taking longer than expected…

What Olav did not know (and unfortunately for them, the vikings did not know either) was that this particular monastery did not brew ale, or gather honey, or bake cakes.

The monks living here were blacksmiths. They spent every afternoon striking heavy hammers against their anvils, fashioning useful things like horseshoes and garden gates and even more hammers. These goods were still stealable, but they were a lot heavier to carry to the ship than cakes, so the plundering was not going as smoothly as the vikings had expected.

The second thing the vikings did not know was that because the monks spent every afternoon swinging heavy hammers (and building up some impressive muscles in the process) they had to get up very early in the morning to squeeze in all their praying and manuscript illustrating. So early the sun had not yet risen. So early, in fact, that the monks had been on their way down to breakfast when the vikings' ship landed, and they had seen the pillagers coming.

The third thing the vikings did not know was that these particular monks had not taken a vow of nonviolence. They had taken a vow of silence instead. And with all that practice keeping quiet they were very, *very* good at sneaking up on people.

Of course Olav didn't know any of that either. All he knew was that his boredom was suddenly interrupted by a lot of yelling and clanging sounds coming from the top of the cliff. It was still dark, and even if the sun had risen he couldn't have seen what was happening way up there, but he craned his neck toward the commotion all the same. While he was distracted, a teenage boy in a monk's habit leaped onto the ship, grabbed an oar, and started paddling backward.

"What are you doing?" Olav hissed at the boy.

The young monk yelled something back in a language Olav couldn't understand and kept right on rowing.

Normally it took more than a dozen vikings to crew the ship. Olav doubted one boy would be able to steal it all on his own. But while the vikings were gone the tide had come in, so the ship was no longer moored in the sand. In no time at all the ship was backing away from the shore. By the time the sun started peeking over the horizon the ship was well out to sea, taking Olav and the runaway monk with it.

Olav wasn't sure how he'd expected this day to go, but getting kidnapped by an underaged monk certainly hadn't been on the list. But as he didn't know anything about sailing himself, and he wasn't eager to go back and face Captain Sigrid's wrath for letting the ship get stolen, he decided there was no alternative but to go along with whatever the boy had in mind.

When they could no longer see the island, the monk pulled in the oars and unfurled the ship's striped red sail. Now the wind could do all the work for them.

"You sure do know a lot about sailing, for a monk," Olav observed.

The boy held out his hand in a gesture of welcome. "Edric," he said, pointing to himself.

"Olav," said Olav, returning the gesture.

The two unlikely sailors shook hands.

Since the vikings had prepared the ship for a month's journey, there was no shortage of supplies. They had casks of fresh water, and all the salted fish, dried plums, and wayfarer's biscuits they could eat. But though Edric seemed to know his way around the ship's oars and rigging well enough (and had some truly impressive arm muscles, for no reason Olav could explain) they still did not have any way to plan their navigation. Of course, it would help to have some idea where they were going. Since neither of them wanted to be anywhere near the monastery island, all Olav could think to do was return to Björnvald. He didn't know where it was, exactly, except that when leaving the village they'd had the rising sun on their left every morning, so he figured the return trip should put the sunrise on their right. This meant they were heading more or less north, so at night they tried to keep the North Star directly ahead.

Edric was an unusually chatty sailing companion. He didn't seem to mind that Olav could not understand a word he said; all day long (and well into each night) the boy kept up a constant stream of babbling commentary. They passed the time by teaching each other a few simple words in their respective languages—"fish", "boat", "sail", "seasick"—but there was no explanation necessary when on the fifth day Edric pointed at the prow of the ship, gabbling with excitement.

A raven had landed on the dragon-shaped figurehead. It

was soon followed by another, which perched on the sail's crossbeam. Olav knew exactly what Edric was so excited about. Ravens meant they were nearing land.

But where was it? Olav was certain ravens never ventured too far from shore, but all he could see in every direction was cold, gray ocean.

Dark clouds rolled in from the horizon. Lightning flashed in the distance. A storm was brewing, and from the looks of things it would soon overtake them. But the ravens remained perched on the ship. Surely, Olav thought, they'd prefer to ride out a storm on land?

The ravens kept to their posts.

Edric gathered up the sail and lashed down anything he couldn't stow in the ship's hold. The looming clouds grew closer and darker. Then the wind picked up, pelting their faces with cold rain.

The ravens didn't budge.

The gale soon reached ferocious intensity. The sea broke into hungry waves, tossing the ship like a child's toy. Just when Olav was sure the storm would swallow their ship whole, there was a flash of light. Not lightning, this time—it was as though the sun itself leaned in from the heavens for a closer view of the ship's plight, forcing the desperate sailors to shield their eyes from its brilliant rays.

And then the light was gone. When Olav and Edric opened their eyes again, they realized the storm was gone too. Their ship was floating in calm, peaceful waters not a stone's throw from land.

Their raven passengers took flight over the pebbly beach and disappeared into the mass of alder trees lining the ridge beyond it. "Thank you," said Olav quietly as he watched the birds fly off. "Send Odin our regards." He knew they could not hear him, but it didn't matter. He was certain the ravens' presence was the only thing that had allowed them to survive the storm.

Lucky birds aside, Olav could think of no explanation for the sudden conclusion to so fierce a gale. But what troubled him more was that surely, no storm was fierce enough to hide an entire landmass at such close range. It was as though the beach had appeared out of nowhere.

This was not Björnvald. There were no houses, no shipyard, no village green filled with noisy children's games. The only sound was that of gentle waves lapping against the side of the ship, punctuated by Edric's indecipherable running commentary.

Edric secured a line around the ship's figurehead, then splashed his way to shore and fastened the other end to a massive boulder. Olav followed, and together they set to work exploring.

———

Olav and Edric found a river that emptied out to the bay where their ship had come to rest. Knowing that people tended to congregate near fresh water, they decided to follow it back to its source. Perhaps, Olav hoped, if they found a village, he could ask for navigation instructions back to Björnvald. They had been sailing north for five days already. With any luck, they had returned to lands that spoke his language and might be familiar with the other settlements nearby. But though he and Edric walked for hours, they found no sign of people. Not only was the forested landscape devoid of active villages, there were no signs people had *ever* set foot there. No moss-covered abandoned cabins. No ax-cut tree stumps. No blackened campfire pits. Not even the litter of long-broken cooking pots, or messages like "Ingmar was here" and "Sven + Helga 4 Evr" scrawled on boulders and carved into tree trunks.

They returned to the ship that night and set out the next morning with a new plan: if the land could not support population, then perhaps it was only a tiny island. They would walk all the way around its edge and see if they could spot a larger landmass on the other side. But again, though they walked for hours, they found no sign of human habitation, and the rocky beach stretched on seemingly endlessly without curving around to meet itself. Wherever they had landed, it now seemed certain: it was empty, and it was *big*.

The only feature of real interest they encountered was the blackened husk of a tree that had been split right down the center, tip to trunk, splintering into three long arms that now reached across the beach instead of toward the sky. Olav had seen this before, back in Björnvald. Only one force could slice such a mighty oak so cleanly. It must have been struck by lightning.

He spotted something glistening at the base and wandered over to inspect it. He picked it up: a jagged black stone as large as his fist, its surface sparkling with a metallic sheen as though it was coated in morning dew.

Olav had never seen anything like it. He passed the rock over to Edric, who babbled enthusiastically while turning it over in his fingers to examine every angle. But when the boy brought the stone up to his face for a closer look, a strange thing happened.

Edric wore around his neck a long, thin leather cord, on which hung an iron pendant—some childhood souvenir, Olav imagined, or perhaps a lucky charm. Normally he wore it tucked under his monk's habit, but when he drew the strange black rock close the leather cord snaked itself out from the neck of his robe. The pendant strained at the end of its tether, floating unsupported in the air as if reaching desperately for the rock.

For the first time since Olav met the boy, Edric had nothing to say. He only removed the necklace and dangled it over the strange stone. No matter where he moved the stone, the metal pendant followed it. When he finally brought the necklace close enough to touch the rock, the pendant clung to its side like they'd been welded together in a forge.

Olav's first thought was that this must be some kind of evil omen. But on reflection, he decided the opposite was more likely. If a luck token was drawn to the stone, then surely it must also be lucky. He pried the pendant away from it, returned the necklace to Edric, and put the stone in his pocket. He wasn't sure how, but Olav had a feeling this strange rock might someday prove useful.

——————

Zed turned the page, but the back side was blank. The heading on the next page was for a completely different story.

"That's *it?*" Tuesday snatched the book out of Zed's hands and flipped through the pages for herself. "Where's the rest of it?"

Zed shrugged. "Don't look at me. *I* didn't write it."

"It doesn't even make any sense!" Tuesday turned her outrage on Bastian. "*This* is what passes for a history book around here? The story doesn't even explain how Olav got to be a Waymaster, much less a founder of Falinnheim."

Bastian threw his hands up in defense. "I'm just as confused as you are."

"That magnetic rock sounds just like the lodestone we got in the market on our first day in Falinnheim," Zed mused aloud. "From the chemist's stall, remember?"

Tuesday remembered. But she was too worked up at the moment to be agreeable. "That dumb rock was the weirdest part of all," she complained. "The book makes it sound like Olav and Edric had never heard of magnets before. Magnetism is like the first real science thing they talk about in *kindergarten*. It's not exactly rocket science, you know?"

Bastian raised an eyebrow at her. "What's a rocket?"

"Never mind," said Zed, taking the book back from Tuesday and passing it over to give Bastian a turn. "We'll just have to keep reading."

CHAPTER 9
THE TALE OF EDRIC THE WORDY

The tale of Edric the Wordy begins long before he was called that. In the beginning, he was as un-wordy as it is possible to be. In fact, Edric did not know any words at all, because he was a baby.

Besides not knowing how to talk yet (or much of anything else, really) Edric also did not know that he had a problem. You see, Edric had an older brother, Alfred.

Alfred and Edric lived with their parents in a lavish manor. It was not quite a castle, but it was certainly not a thatched hut, which is where most of the villagers of Therwick Green went to sleep every night. Growing up in a fancy house with servants and fine clothes and meat on the table every night might seem like the *opposite* of a problem, but the fact was that since Alfred was the family's firstborn son, he would someday inherit the entire estate.

Edric the Baby would soon become Edric the Grown Man, and then he would be left with nothing.

Edric's father did not seem terribly concerned about this. After all, he was a firstborn son himself, and when he'd inherited this estate, his younger brothers had (probably) turned out fine, wherever they ended up. But Edric's mother was not so content. She could not sleep peacefully knowing that one of her sons would someday become a wealthy landowner, and the other would be sent packing like some unwelcome peddler. But she could not change the law, and she could not inherit the property herself. So at last she devised a plan: she would place Edric in the care of the monastery on the nearby island of Lindisfarne. She would have to contribute a hefty sum to the monastery's coffers, but they would not turn away a nobleman's son. At least as a monk Edric would have a respected profession, a roof over his head, and better meals than the gruel and foraged mushrooms the villagers lived on.

Edric the Baby soon grew into Edric the Boy, and he had an idyllic childhood running through the barley fields with Alfred, playing Hoodman's Bluff and plunking stones in the millpond. But eventually, Edric the Boy became Edric the Youth. The time for play was at an end.

No one thought to consult Edric about his future. Everything was already arranged. As a monk, he would be expected to renounce all personal possessions, so there was no need to even pack a trunk for his journey. His parents simply waved from the shore as the ferry master rowed him across the bay to his new home on the monastery island.

Alfred watched from the shore too, but he did not wave. He saw no reason they shouldn't just split the inheritance when the time came, or perhaps build a second large house right next to the first one so he and his brother could be neighbors. But no one thought to consult Alfred either.

The first rule: obedience. Edric would be where and when the supervising monks directed, no questions asked.

The second rule: diligence. Whatever the task at hand, Edric would devote every effort to its skillful completion, no questions asked.

The third rule: silence. Always, silence. This was why there would be no questions asked.

Despite this austere environment, life at the monastery was not all bad. Though the monks insisted that spoken conversation distracted from the more vital pursuits of reverent study and contemplation, for the most part they were cheerful and pleasant companions, always eager to exchange an encouraging wave or a written note. The monastery itself was comfortable and well kept, and its library was positively luxurious. Edric had thought his father's household richly privileged to be in possession of three entire books, but the scope of the monastery's wealth left him speechless. (Or at least it would have, if he'd been allowed to speak.) There were books, scrolls, maps, and parchments tucked into every available nook and corner, shelf and cupboard.

His childhood tutor had already taught him to read and write in English, but through his daily work copying ancient manuscripts and memorizing sacred texts, he soon learned Latin and Greek as well. The monks had even devised their own collection of hand signals to get around the need for conversation, and it was not long before Edric mastered this language too.

Aside from languages, Edric was also instructed in geography, history, philosophy, theology, and art. And when all this study made him restless, that was the perfect opportunity to head out to the workshop and throw his bottled-up energy into mastering the monks' blacksmithing trade. In three short years, he learned to forge everything from farm plows to gate hinges.

Yes, he missed his family, but all told, life at the monastery was going pretty well for young Edric. Which is why he decided it was time to leave.

If he didn't talk to someone soon, he was certain he'd go absolutely mad.

———

"Yeah, yeah, we get it," Tuesday interrupted. "Edric doesn't want to live at the monastery anymore, so when the vikings show up he jumps into Olav's boat and escapes. Skip ahead to something we *don't* know."

Zed glared at her. "There's a lot more to a story than

knowing how it *ends,*" he argued. "Whoever translated and compiled all these histories put a lot of work into making them more interesting than some boring old textbook, and I for one want to hear how—"

But Bastian had already turned the page.

———

Edric didn't know much about sailing, but the redheaded viking seemed to know even less, if that was possible. He was relieved that Olav hadn't tried to stop him from taking the ship (or waited until they were far from shore and then thrown him into the ocean.) But if they were going to be in this adventure together, a little help now and then would be nice. He wasn't entirely convinced that what little he'd read about ships in the monastery's library would be enough to pull off a successful voyage. But then, he hadn't expected anyone to be on board at all, in which case he'd have been doing all the work himself anyway. At least now he had someone to talk to.

He tried to teach Olav a few simple words—"fish", "boat", "sail", "seasick"—but the young viking didn't seem any more interested in learning English, Greek, or Latin than he was in learning to sail. Olav rarely said much at all, even in his native Norse. Edric did catch Olav singing a time or two, though, which made him smile as he worked. He couldn't understand the lyrics, but the viking's singing voice wasn't half bad.

The journey progressed without incident until the fifth

day, when an unwelcome omen landed right on their prow. A raven perched on the dragon-shaped figurehead, staring Edric down with its ominous, beady black eyes.

Edric sucked in a breath. Everyone knew ravens were bad luck. They tended to congregate where something had died—or was *about* to—and having one show up with no land in sight could *not* be a good sign.

Another raven joined the first, settling in on the mast. Edric tried to point this out to Olav, but as usual, the viking said nothing.

Edric's fears were confirmed when a storm gathered on the horizon. It was as though the ravens had brought the wind and lightning with them.

He *knew* those evil birds were up to no good.

———

Tuesday sighed loudly and rolled her eyes in Bastian's direction.

Bastian got the message. He flipped another page. "Let's see… ravens, storm, bright light, no storm, land, exploring, find the lightning tree… ah, here we go!"

———

Edric wore around his neck a long, thin leather cord, on which hung an iron pendant shaped like a miniature horseshoe. He had fashioned it himself when he first began to learn blacksmithing at the monastery. After an entire week of disastrous attempts at making full-sized horseshoes, Brother Cuthbert had demoted Edric to crafting simpler hardware.

Unwilling to give up, Edric had persisted, practicing the technique on discarded nails. When he finally turned out a horseshoe he was proud of, he slapped it defiantly down on the older monk's anvil, and Brother Cuthbert had chuckled and clapped his apprentice on the back so enthusiastically at seeing its craftsmanship that Edric had kept the miniature version as a hard-won trophy.

Normally Edric wore the necklace tucked under his monk's habit, but when he drew the glistening black rock close, the leather cord snaked itself out from the neck of his robe. The tiny horseshoe strained at the end of its tether, floating unsupported in the air as if reaching desperately for the rock.

Could it be? Edric removed the cord and dangled it over the stone. No matter where he moved the stone, the horseshoe followed it. When he finally brought the necklace close enough to touch the rock, the horseshoe clung to its side like they'd been welded together in a forge.

He had read about lodestones, of course. The ancient Greek philosopher Thales of Miletus had proposed the mineral's properties as evidence that it had a soul, which the monks had vigorously debated (in writing, of course) on theological grounds. But he had never expected he'd actually see one.

Edric wanted to explain this to his companion—surely he could find some way to mime what he was getting at, language barrier or not—but the viking was as quiet and sullen as always. Olav merely snatched the rock, tossed the necklace back, then stuffed the lodestone into his pocket.

Edric sighed. He wanted more time to experiment with the sample, but it would have to wait. After all, he had already commandeered Olav's entire ship. If letting the grumpy viking keep track of their find kept the peace, he supposed that was only fair.

———

They had sailed too far north, that was the problem. Edric was sure of it. He didn't understand much Norse, but he'd been able to piece together enough of Olav's limited conversation to gather they were headed back to his village. Edric couldn't go home—his family would just send him back to the monastery—so this plan seemed as good as any. Besides, it would feel less like stealing if he helped get the viking ship back where it came from. If they'd made it to lands that had never been settled, it must be because the extreme northern climate would be too harsh, come winter. Clearly, they were much too far north. All they had to do was head south for a while. They'd spot Björnvald in no time.

After refilling their water casks and gathering all the wild brambleberries they could find, Edric and Olav unmoored the ship and set out at the next high tide. But before they'd even left the sheltered bay, it happened again: a bright light enveloped the ship, just as it had during the storm. By the time the light receded enough for them to see their surroundings the ship was bobbing along in the open ocean, with no land in sight.

Edric couldn't blame this strange occurrence on the ravens this time, since the foul birds were no longer on board. But clearly, something very odd was at work.

They couldn't have overshot Björnvald by very much, Edric decided. One day's sailing, maybe a day and a half, should at least put them in sight of the correct coastline. But before the sun had even risen to its midday height, they spotted not the inlets and fjords of the Nordic coastline but a sandy beach lined with some variety of tree they'd never seen before. The curving trunk formed one tall, bare column topped with shaggy green fronds that stuck out as wildly as Olav's uncombed hair. The ship's striped sail caught not the frigid winds of the North Sea, but breezes so warm that Olav and Edric were soon forced to remove their outermost layer of clothing to keep cool.

Edric adjusted the sails to head toward land, and by sunset he was pulling out the oars to row the last stretch to a small island. When they lodged in the sand, he splashed ashore and threw a rigging line around one of the strange trees to anchor the ship.

He was just tugging the knot into place when the guards arrived.

Well, it was only *one* guard, at least at first. A young woman had crept up behind Edric while he anchored the ship and was now pointing a large knife toward his ribs in a rather threatening manner.

"We're not really vikings," Edric tried to explain, thinking the ship's distinctive appearance had given her the wrong impression. "See, we're running *away* from the vikings. We only want directions—we're not here to steal."

The woman did not seem convinced. Her eyebrows scrunched together, creasing her bronze face into a menacing mask, but she said nothing.

Olav was no help at all, of course. He stood frozen on the ship's deck, staring indecisively between Edric and his captor, then raised his hands to show he was unarmed.

Perhaps she couldn't understand him? Edric decided to try Latin. He had no idea where the ship had landed, but enough languages were based on Latin that perhaps she would recognize a word or two.

The woman's scowl deepened.

Greek? Edric tried again and glanced hopefully from Olav to the angry guard, who gripped her knife still tighter and jabbed it impatiently toward him.

Apparently not.

Desperate to defuse the situation, Edric launched into the only form of communication he had left: the monks' hand signals. He signed a boat, rain, and wind; drew one finger along his flattened palm, to indicate a map; then closed his fist and moved it quickly to one side, as if balling up the map and throwing it away. Finally he pointed to himself, Olav, and the woman in turn, then shook hands with himself. *There was a storm. We are lost. We are friends.*

The woman's eyebrows twitched even closer together, and her frown deepened still further. But it seemed her anger had evaporated. She tilted her head slightly and stared hard into his eyes, as though seeing him for the first time. Then, slowly, she lowered her weapon to the sand and signed back.

Her signals were unfamiliar to Edric. The monks had developed their hand symbols among themselves, so naturally no one outside the monastery would use precisely the same gestures. But many of them were intuitive enough that he felt he understood.

You can hear?

Edric nodded.

Your friend cannot sign?

Edric shook his head.

Who taught you?

Edric plucked at his monk's robe, then made the sign for prayer.

That seemed to be enough for her. The woman returned her knife to its sheath, beckoned Olav down from the ship's deck, and led the way across the beach.

———

This time, there were *lots* of guards. The woman led Edric and Olav up wide stone steps, past fluted columns and spear-toting sentries, into the cool, dim interior of a massive building carved entirely from white marble. They had passed plenty of other buildings along the way, but those were made of rough sandstone bricks. This one made Edric's childhood manor look like an outhouse. This one was a palace.

Their guide marched up a long, echoing aisle lined with staring courtiers to the far end of the largest room, where an old man sat on an ornately carved chair, silently reading a scroll of parchment. He didn't seem to notice her approach. He chuckled to himself as he read, occasionally reaching for the bunch of grapes on a nearby side table and popping one into his mouth.

After waiting before him for an awkward length of time, the woman clapped loudly, then folded her arms.

The man looked up. He smiled, set his parchment down next to the grapes, and began signing to her. They conversed in a silent flurry of hand signals that was far too rapid and complicated for Edric to follow. Then the woman stood aside and motioned Edric forward.

Edric promptly began to panic. He couldn't hope to communicate in any signs so sophisticated! The monks' gestures were mostly a shortcut for everyday pleasantries, but clearly this land had created an entire language of them. Even if he managed to convince the man that he and Olav meant no harm, how could he possibly ask for directions?

While Edric was busy worrying, the old man stood up, smoothed his long salt-and-pepper beard, and addressed the newcomers. "Welcome, strangers!" he said in perfect Greek. "It appears you've had quite the adventure. Care to tell us your story?"

<hr>

"Let me guess," Tuesday groaned. "That's the end of the chapter?"

"Yup," said Bastian.

"We're gonna have to read all about the next character's life before we get back to the action, aren't we?" Zed guessed.

Bastian shrugged. "Probably."

Tuesday took another bite of her sandwich. "Let's get on with it, then."

CHAPTER 10
THE TALE OF SELENE THE NEGOTIATOR

The tale of Cyril the Librarian begins with a library, a fire, and a daring plan.

This story is not about Cyril. But all stories are connected, just as all people are, so this is where we must begin. We'll get to Selene in a minute.

Long, *long* before Cyril's story began, a man named Alexander ruled the world. At least, that's what Alexander decided to tell everyone. In reality, he didn't even *know* about most of the world, let alone run it. But Alexander came from a long line of kings and was the student of a long line of philosophers and generals, each with their own roots in legendary tales of heroism and greatness. The only way young Alexander could see to take his place among their stories was to create one of his own. So when he'd finished taking over all the lands and kingdoms he knew about, he proclaimed those were all the lands that existed.

Alexander was an ambitious man, but not a terribly creative one, so the title he took to celebrate his achievements was simply Alexander the Great. (A better name than Alexander the Adequate, you must admit. But still—not the most original.) He became king of Macedon at the age of twenty, and by the age of thirty he was king of Greece, Babylon, Persia, and Egypt as well. And by the age of thirty-two, he was dead.

He was called Alexander the Great, not Alexander the Healthy and Long-lived.

This story is not about Alexander either.

The only reason we mention Alexander at all is that one of his many schemes to spread the story of his greatness was to build grand cities in the lands he conquered and name them after himself. When he declared himself Pharaoh of Egypt, he ordered the construction of yet another of these grand cities and decreed it would be called Alexandria.

He had already named several other cities in his empire "Alexandria"—once again, he was not called Alexander the Imaginative—but this one was the most famous. He died before ever setting foot there, but no matter. The next pharaoh carried on without him. The Egyptian port of Alexandria was soon home to the world's tallest lighthouse and a museum hosting the world's greatest scholars. But perhaps its most famous feature was its massive library, which claimed to have a copy of every book in the world.

This is where our librarian comes in.

Being named Royal Librarian was among Alexandria's highest honors, a post appointed by the pharaoh himself. In addition to managing the library's ever-growing collection of records, the librarian was the head scholar of the museum's academics and private tutor to the children in the pharaoh's household. For hundreds of years, the librarians of Alexandria passed the title from one steward to the next, each scouring incoming ships for new books to add to their collection and organizing the incalculable number of documents for easy retrieval and study. The library's prestige made Alexandria a hub of the cultural elite, home to Greeks and Egyptians, Jews and Muslims, Christians and Pagans. The museum's scholars used the library's collected knowledge to make massive leaps in the study of mathematics, astronomy, geography, medicine, engineering, and literature.

That is, until the fire.

When Caesar's ships sailed into Alexandria's port and burned the Egyptian fleet, the blaze spread to the rest of the city, which posed a definite problem for a collection of notoriously flammable scrolls and books. The city managed to put the fire out before losing the library's entire collection, but they couldn't save everything.

Losing irreplaceable knowledge was bad enough, but the gravest threat wasn't against the books. The real tragedy was that the library suddenly found itself under attack as an institution. First the Romans took over, stealing and renaming the parts of Greek culture they liked and discarding the rest. Then came the Christians, who couldn't stand that women were allowed to study in the library; they even had one female mathematician murdered. Then the Muslim caliphs took their turn. Every time control of Alexandria changed hands, the new leaders viewed its library as a threat, rather than an asset. Any records that didn't align with their worldview and values had to be eliminated. The library's collection began to shrink, instead of grow. Instead of collecting *all* the world's books, soon only the politicians' favorites were welcome.

In the beginning, losing books to the fires of Caesar's war had seemed a devastating tragedy. Now, Alexandria's own were burning the books on purpose.

By the time Cyril took up the post of Royal Librarian he worried he might be the last. Maybe it would be safer to resign his post and leave the politicians to their folly. But he couldn't abandon the library, his life's work, to its destruction. So he formed a daring plan: if the library wasn't welcome in Alexandria, he would simply have to take it somewhere else.

After joining Cyril in a vow of secrecy, the library's scholars set to work. The cartographers searched their maps for a suitable new home. The engineers designed and commissioned ships. The philosophers gave impassioned speeches to all the city's citizens who could be persuaded to join their cause. And all the rest got to work gathering supplies and carefully packing up the books and scrolls. When everything was ready, three hundred people boarded their ships, waited for nightfall, and sailed away from Alexandria's shore, never to return.

The refugees settled on the island the cartographers had selected, nestled into a forgotten patch of the Mediterranean Sea. It was large enough to support their needs, but small enough that it didn't appear on most maps. Especially not on the outdated maps Alexandria's leaders had access to, because they no longer had a library.

––––––––

Decades passed. The scholars built new homes and a new library. Cyril the Librarian tended his people and his books with equal care. Occasionally the island was visited by merchant sailors on their way to other ports, but Alexandria's soldiers never came looking for them (or if they did, they never succeeded.) This was likely because Cyril declined to give the island a name and forbade its inclusion on any of the library's maps. When visiting sailors told others about the island, their descriptions were too vague to raise any suspicions.

Everything seemed to be going fine. That is, until the sickness came.

Perhaps it arrived on one of those merchant ships. Or perhaps people's humors got out of balance. Whatever the reason, in the thirty-first year of Cyril's leadership, a fever swept the island. The medical scholars tried everything from leeches to herb poultices, but nothing seemed to help. People either banished the fever on their own, or they didn't. The island's population had grown to over five hundred by that time, but fifty-six of those were lost to the sickness.

Three weeks later it was over. Cyril recovered, but now he had a new problem. The sickness had claimed all the adults in some households, leaving only children behind. He had sixteen orphans to find homes for. Neighbors and friends stepped in where they could, and soon homes were found for the oldest fifteen. But one child remained, a baby, who no one came forward to claim.

There was only one thing left to do: Cyril decided to adopt the tiny girl himself. At the age of sixty-three, Cyril the Librarian became a father.

He named the baby Selene.

———

Cyril soon discovered that babies do not remain babies for long. Almost overnight, it seemed, Selene grew into a toddler, and then a child. Before he knew it, she was running around the island, scuttling up palm trees and playing hide-and-seek in the endless shelves of the new library. But though she was the joy of his advancing years and the light of each day, Cyril eventually had to admit that his daughter had one limitation. Though she had cried as a baby and shrieked and giggled as a toddler, Selene never spoke a single word.

The doctors determined that the fever had taken her hearing, and since she could not hear others speaking, she never learned to imitate them. But Cyril decided this was no problem; after all, he was getting on in years, and his own hearing was not what it used to be. They would simply have to find some other way to communicate.

It was Selene herself who came up with the solution. One day as she was walking along the beach with her father, she saw a flock of seagulls. She pointed them out to him, and then flapped her arms to imitate the birds.

"Why not?" Cyril said to himself. "Why can't a word be an action, instead of a sound?" He repeated her flapping motion and pointed at the gulls.

Selene beamed up at him. She knew Dad understood. But all that arm flapping was getting tiring. She decided to try a similar motion using only her hands, bringing her thumbs together and spreading the rest of her fingers outward like wings.

Cyril watched the girl carefully, then copied her sign and pointed at the birds again. Selene nodded, satisfied he had learned her new invention, and skipped down the beach to hunt for seashells.

There were dozens of others on the island who had trouble hearing since the fever came, but because they were older they had already learned to speak, read, and write. Mostly they had taken to carrying chalk and small slates with them, but a way to talk with their hands would be much more convenient than writing. They eagerly accepted Cyril's challenge to develop an entire language of hand signals. The friends and family members of the island's new Deaf Scholars Society needed to communicate with them, so it was not long before everyone, hearing or not, used at least a few signs.

Selene was an eager student, but though she learned to read and write as seamlessly as she signed, she never outgrew her boundless energy. She would much rather spend her days climbing trees and scanning the sea for passing ships than cooped up in the library with her father. So when Selene reached the age of apprenticeship, she decided to join the island's defense league. Which is how she happened to be on lookout duty the day a most unusual ship arrived.

A ship that looked like a dragon.

————

"*Finally!*" Tuesday exclaimed. "Now we can skip to the action!"

Zed rolled his eyes. "World conquerors, wars, fires, book banning, a sneaky escape, and a deadly plague weren't enough action for you?"

"You know what I mean," she said. "Olav, Edric, and Selene have finally met. We know how each of their stories got started. Now we can find out what any of it has to do with Falinnheim."

Bastian nodded, flipped forward a couple pages, and

picked up where Edric's story had left off.

————

Edric nearly swallowed his tongue. Greek? He had tried the language on the guard mostly out of desperation, but now he realized how ridiculous that was. It was over two thousand miles from the monastery island to Greece, and that was the direct path over land. To get there by sea they would have to sail all the way around France and Spain, but they had only left the mysterious empty land (which was even further north than the monastery) this morning. It simply wasn't possible.

Edric had a lot more practice reading Greek than speaking it, but no matter how bad his grammar came out, it would definitely be easier than attempting to sign. He took a breath to steady his nerves and addressed the man on the throne, explaining that they were lost at sea, meant no harm, and simply needed directions back to Olav's village so they could return the "borrowed" ship.

Cyril introduced himself, welcomed his visitors, and called for a map to be brought up from the archives.

Olav didn't pay much attention to the proceedings. He was far too busy staring at the woman who had captured them, wearing a rather dreamy expression. Edric rolled his eyes. Leave it to the viking to get distracted at a time like this…

Three servants returned toting a massive map on their shoulders, rolled up like a Persian rug. They laid it out on the floor and Cyril stepped down from his seat to inspect it.

"We are… *here*," he said, pointing out the blank space of ocean where the island would belong, if the map included it. "Where are you trying to go?"

Edric stared. He and Olav weren't off the coast of Greece at all. They had come even further—nearly all the way to Egypt.

With a sigh, Edric walked to the map's top corner, past Britain, and pointed to the far edge of the North Sea. This was as close as he could get, because Björnvald did not appear on the map at all.

Cyril smiled sadly at the lost young man. "I'm truly sorry," he said. "I cannot help you sail to lands past the edge of the map."

"What should we do, then?" asked Edric.

"Never fear," Cyril replied. "The Library of Alexandria welcomes all new additions to its collection. People included."

Between the library's scholars there were people who could speak Greek, Latin, Coptic, Arabic, Hebrew, and Aramaic. Edric was able to get his point across well enough in Greek or Latin, but he really wished someone there understood English so he could express himself more freely. No one understood any Norse at all, aside from the few words Olav and Edric had taught each other on the ship. So Cyril suggested a compromise: the easiest way to get everyone on equal footing was for the newcomers to learn to sign. And since he was always looking for a good excuse to get his daughter back into the library (and off of the beach, where she'd inevitably revert to climbing palm trees and threatening visiting sailors) he volunteered Selene to be their tutor.

Selene was *not* happy about this new assignment. She wasn't sure whether her father was solely interested in her signing fluency or perhaps secretly wanted her to keep an eye on the mysterious invaders. Either way, she considered babysitting duty an insult to her skills. But though she argued with Cyril all the time as her father, she could not disobey his orders as the Librarian. So the next morning (and every morning after), Olav, Edric and Selene met in the library and got to work.

Edric's natural talent for languages served him well, but he could not compete with Olav. To the monk's astonishment, the reluctant viking took to signing like a thief takes to gold. He hadn't shown any particular interest in learning English, but something about this language of signs (or, perhaps, his tutor) seemed to light a fire in Olav. In a matter of months, Edric and Olav had progressed enough in their studies that they were finally able to share their separate stories before fate brought them together. And in time, Selene let her guard down enough to share her stories, too.

Olav and Edric stayed. They studied with the library's scholars, poring over maps and history books, and recounting their adventures to the scribes so their records could be added to the library's collection. Edric traded in his monk's habit for the simple draped linen everyone else on the island wore (which was fortunate, because at the rate his height was shooting up, he would soon have outgrown his old clothes anyway). Olav no longer worried about being forced into a life of seafaring thievery, but he was still particular about keeping his unruly red hair combed (especially before heading to the library to see Selene). The sense of urgency to return to Björnvald gradually faded, as did Edric and Olav's curiosity about the strange empty land and the unexplainable circumstances that had brought their ship so far from it so quickly. Before they knew it two years had passed. Though Olav and Edric no longer needed tutoring, they kept finding excuses to join Selene in the library each morning. And to her surprise, Selene realized this did not bother her one bit.

The three friends might have gone on like this forever if the scholars hadn't discovered the emergency.

The library's greatest minds brought their findings to Cyril. They could not explain why, but there was no denying the evidence. Their island was gradually sinking. The tides were rising higher and higher every week, and several guard posts along the shore had been claimed by the sea already. By the scholars' calculations, in less than a year the entire island would be underwater.

"We brought everyone here by ship," Cyril proclaimed. "We can do it again."

The Librarian tried to put up a determined front for his people, but privately, he knew it would not be so easy. True, they had made a sea voyage and found a new home once before. But that had been fifty-three years ago. His people now numbered nearly one thousand, more than three times the population at the island's founding. Even if they were willing to start their lives again from scratch, where could he possibly find enough space for so many people?

Fortunately, Olav had the perfect place in mind. He just had to figure out how to get there.

———

And that was the end of the chapter.

"*Typical*," Tuesday seethed, tossing aside her empty plate. "We finally get to a woman's story, and the book spends the entire time talking about the men around her, instead. Selene was barely even in this one!"

"Well, it's a history book," Zed offered, trying to soothe his sister's temper. "There usually aren't many women in those. Not the ones about ancient history, anyway."

"Can you even *hear* yourself?" she snapped. "Women are half the planet! Their lives are half of all the stuff that happened in history. There is *nothing normal* about their stories going missing. If they aren't included in history books, it's because the people writing them decided to leave women out and focus on men's stories instead. It's not like women didn't contribute anything important—historians deliberately ignored them."

"Hey, there were a bunch of cool women in ancient history!" Zed backpedaled. "Like… Marie Antionette."

"She was famous for getting *murdered,*" Tuesday reminded him. "There's nothing cool about that."

"Okay… Joan of Arc," he tried next.

"Murdered."

"Sacagawea?"

"Literally sold as property, and the only part of her life people ever talk about is how she helped famous men not die."

Bastian nearly had to yell to break up the argument. "It says Selene's in the next chapter too," he pointed out. "Let's keep reading and see what happens."

"Fine," Tuesday huffed as she snatched the book from Bastian's hands. "But *I'm* reading this one. And if Selene doesn't get properly celebrated, I am *done* with this dumb book."

CHAPTER 11
THE TALE OF THE THREE FOUNDERS

Selene, Edric, and Olav met in the library as usual, but this morning's study session was not business as usual at all. Instead of letting Selene pilot the discussion, this time Olav kicked off the day's study. And instead of gathering books and scrolls to consult, today he pulled a large, sparkly black rock out of his pocket and placed it reverently in the center of the table.

I know where to move everyone, Olav signed. *It's not an island, so it can't sink or get washed away by storms. And there's no one living there to bother us. The library will be safe.*

It's the perfect place! Edric agreed. *But what's that got to do with the lodestone?*

This stone is a piece of the hidden land. I think our ship moved so strangely because we had the stone with us. We can use it to find our way back. It's like a key to an invisible door.

We didn't have the lodestone when we found the land the first time, Edric argued.

The ravens let us in that time, Olav insisted. *We didn't need the stone then.*

Edric responded with a face of utter contempt. He wasn't about to give those creepy carrion scavengers credit for anything.

Just show her, Olav urged.

Edric rolled his eyes, but dutifully removed the horseshoe pendant from around his neck and waved it over the table, demonstrating how the metal reached for the lodestone no matter where he moved the cord.

Selene frowned. *Is the hidden land made of iron too?* she signed. *What makes you think the rock will lead us there?*

Olav shrugged. Who knew why the stone behaved so oddly? All he knew was that he'd never seen any other rock with magic powers. The fact that it came from a land that seemed to be tucked in a separate pocket from the rest of the world couldn't be a coincidence.

Selene pulled a loose string from the hem of her dress and tied it around the stone. She left enough string dangling after the knot to hold the rock up, just as Edric had suspended the horseshoe. Now the horseshoe and the rock both tugged at the ends of their tethers, reaching for each other. But then something unexpected happened. When she and Edric moved far enough from each other that the stone and iron were out of range, the lodestone twisted itself around on its string. Though the stone now dropped straight down instead of reaching through the air, it also rotated so that one particularly jagged point always faced toward the library door. No matter which direction she moved, even if she spun the stone around, it always settled back to point out the door.

See? Olav signed excitedly. *It wants us to go!*

Selene definitely preferred adventure over research, but she was not a librarian's daughter for nothing. It would be ridiculous to plan such an important voyage while sitting in the world's largest library and not at least check what the books had to say on the subject. So with the help of the reference librarian on duty, she located all the records mentioning lodestones and hauled them back to the table.

After hours of research, they learned that Alexander the Great made his soldiers carry lodestones to protect them from evil spirits (kind of weird) and that the ancient Greeks used to carve statues of their gods out of lodestone and hold ceremonial weddings for the statues that were drawn to each other (*very* weird). In fact, only one of the records seemed at all helpful. It mentioned a traveling merchant from the east who had a lodestone carved in the shape of a fish. When placed in a bowl of water, the fish always faced south. The only exception came when his ship sailed past a strange island that did not appear on their navigational charts. For the entire day they sailed past, the lodestone fish turned in its bowl and pointed at the island instead.

That gave Olav an idea. He took a piece of chalk from the library's writing slate collection and used it to mark the jagged bit of his lodestone that had seemed to point out the door earlier. He dangled the stone from its string and gave it a spin. Sure enough, when it finished spinning and came to rest the chalked corner pointed toward the doorway.

Which direction is that? he signed to Selene.

Though Selene was familiar with her father's maps, she preferred to tell direction by the stars and the pattern of the winds. None of those were helpful inside a building. So she motioned for the boys to follow her out the door, through the halls, down the library steps, and past the surrounding village to the beach. She knew the island's landscape well enough to navigate it blindfolded. Once they got outside, she wouldn't need a map to know which way was which.

Olav gave the rock another spin and waited for it to settle into position. Sure enough, no matter how he moved, the chalked corner turned to face the sea.

There was just one problem. Unlike the traveler's fish, the corner didn't point south. Selene informed them this beach faced north. But that was better anyway, Edric insisted. North was exactly where they wanted to go.

And when we get close, Olav added, *the stone will point out its home. Just like the traveler's fish pointed out that uncharted island.*

Edric wasn't so confident about that part. But since they had no other ideas, he agreed it was time to present their plan to the Librarian.

____

Three days later Olav and Edric found themselves back on their "borrowed" viking ship, waving to the gathered crowd as they prepared to depart. Not only had the Librarian approved their plan, but he'd stocked their ship with all the maps and provisions the island could spare and insisted they set off immediately to locate the hidden land. Once they could navigate reliably between the two places, everyone else could make the journey in their own ships. In the meantime, he had an entire library to pack up. And since Cyril was too busy packing to oversee the voyage himself, he assigned Selene to accompany them as the Librarian's personal representative.

After giving her father one last hug, Selene boarded the ship, waved to the crowd, and set to work helping Edric with the sail rigging.

Don't start thinking you're in charge around here, just because you're the Librarian's fancy ambassador, Edric signed to her with a wink.

Of course she's in charge, don't be stupid, Olav chimed in. *I'd follow Selene anywhere.*

Edric rolled his eyes, but he couldn't suppress a knowing grin. Olav pretended he was joking, but the truth was he already spent most of his time looking for excuses to work with the young guard. The shameless way he tagged along wherever Selene went would make lovesick puppies gag.

Selene and Edric each took a set of oars, and soon they rowed the ship away from the beach and out to sea. Olav stationed himself by the dragon's head carving, checking the lodestone for direction.

They made an unlikely crew, Selene thought: a viking who couldn't sail, an ambassador who never spoke, and a thieving monk who couldn't *stop* talking.

She couldn't think of a better team for an adventure.

———

Just as Olav had predicted, the moment they lost sight of the beach there was a blinding flash. When the light receded, they found themselves surrounded by unfamiliar ocean. Another two hours of sailing (by Selene and Edric, of course; Olav claimed he was far too busy navigating to get involved himself) brought them to a small island. The cool cloud cover and windswept cliffs reminded Edric more of his home than Selene's sun-drenched island, but he soon discovered the landscape and weather weren't the only familiar features.

They rowed to shore, and Olav and Edric were just tethering the ship when a gaggle of young children approached. Edric's ears perked up. The children were speaking English! True, the local accent was a bit different from his own, but it was definitely English.

"Who're you?" one towheaded little urchin asked.

The boy next to him squinted up at the ship's figurehead. "What's your dragon's name?"

A girl came along behind them, glanced up at the ship, and nearly dropped the armload of seashells she was carrying. "Is that a princess?" she gasped.

Edric followed the girl's pointing finger. Selene had just emerged from the ship's hold with a waterskin they had planned to refill on shore.

He chuckled. The draped purple linen Selene had on today might look lavish compared to the undyed wool dresses most English peasant women wore, but he knew Selene was anything but regal. The guard was more likely to scramble barefoot up a tree or pull a knife on somebody than hold court.

What's so funny? Olav signed to him.

They think Selene is a princess, Edric explained.

Now it was Olav's turn to gaze with admiration at Selene. *Well, she sort of is,* he signed back. *The Librarian is in charge of his island. That's like being a king, right? And Selene is his only daughter…*

That gave Edric an idea. He knelt on the pebbly shore to face the little girl. "Do you think the adults in your village would like to meet a princess?" he asked.

The girl broke into an ecstatic grin, dumped all her seashells into Edric's lap, and dashed up the path to the village, shouting with excitement the entire way.

What did you tell her? Olav demanded. *She'll bring the whole village, and the adults might not be as friendly.*

They definitely won't be, Edric assured him.

Selene can't even talk to them, Olav pointed out.

Edric smiled. *Exactly.*

After a quick consultation with his friends, Edric put his plan into action. As he had predicted, the adults of the village were less enthusiastic than the little girl about the prospect of strangers on their shore. Particularly strangers in such an unusual ship. They had never dealt with viking raiders before, but they'd heard the tales. A dozen of the village's burliest farmers abandoned their plows and led the rest of the village back to the beach, armed with axes and clubs. And Edric was ready for them, armed with nothing but his words.

"Who are you lot, then?" one of the farmers growled.

Edric stood in front of the ship, arms folded and chin held high, in the most authoritative pose he could muster. "The magnificent Princess Selene graces you with her presence. In her generosity, she demands no token of your favor. She only wishes to observe your settlement before proceeding on her journey."

On the ship's deck, Selene had her chin held high too, posing regally. Or at least, as regally as she could manage from her seat on an overturned fish barrel.

"You mean you want to spy on us!" The next farmer tried to step around Edric and talk to Selene directly, but Edric intercepted him, looking scandalized.

"How dare you address Her Magnificence! The Princess does not converse with commoners. If you wish to pay her compliments, you may pass your messages through me."

Compliments weren't the sort of message the farmer had in mind. He glanced from the spokesman (impressively muscular, it was true, but he was barely more than a lad, and didn't appear to be armed) to the redheaded young man standing behind him (possibly the least intimidating human he'd ever laid eyes on). This so-called princess sure had strange taste in servants. What was going on?

"What kingdom are you visiting from?" another of the villagers asked. The man eyed Selene suspiciously, trying to make sense of the situation. He'd never met any sort of nobility before, at least not anyone more highborn than the local landlord. This stranger certainly looked different than the local women, both in dress and complexion. But somehow, he had expected a princess to be draped in gold and furs, or wearing a jeweled crown.

Edric turned and made a show of signing to Selene, adding in a lot of unnecessary flourishes. Selene nodded silently, passed some signs back, then folded her hands in her lap and gazed at the scenery with an expression of mild interest.

"Her Magnificence hails from a faraway land," Edric explained to the crowd. "A land so sacred it has no name and does not appear on any map. She travels the seas to survey lands that might make suitable trading partners for her father's kingdom."

Now the villagers were in a pickle. In their experience,

the noble classes generally took more than they gave. They had every reason to suspect that "suitable trading partners" might turn out to mean "new people to steal from." But if this foreign princess actually meant what she said, then they might have an opportunity to sell their local honey, cheese, cloth, and grain for actual gold coins instead of the meager barters the landlord offered. And when the landlord realized the peasants had another market option for their goods, he might be willing to raise his payments to compete…

"We have many goods worthy of trade," an old fishwife informed Edric. "What does the Princess offer *us*?"

Again Edric signed to Selene, who motioned Olav forward. He held out his lodestone and demonstrated how it worked, spinning the rock on its string and allowing it to settle back into place.

"The Princess bestows a gift," Edric announced to the crowd. He took another rock from the shore and bashed it against one end of the lodestone, chipping off a small shard, which he handed to the little girl who'd called them all there. "This stone is imbued with the power of direction. Simply tie it on a string or place it in a dish of water and it will always point north. Then you can navigate to other villages without need of landmarks, and without a clear night for the North Star to point your way."

The girl squealed with delight and hugged the present, then pulled a loose string from her dress and tied it to mimic Olav's larger lodestone. As Edric had promised, the pointed end of the shard faced the same direction as the chalked corner on Olav's stone, no matter how she turned it.

There was a murmur of appreciation from the crowd. Suddenly the idea of a strange unmapped kingdom with novel goods to trade sounded a lot more plausible. If even their rocks were magic, who knew what other useful things they might have to offer?

The townsfolk agreed to show Selene and her "servants" around their village, refilling her waterskin at the well and offering samples of honey, cheese, and dried fish to show off their quality. After complimenting every barley field they passed and eating enough samples to fill the stomach of a bear, the three visitors boarded their dragon-headed ship and sailed off, waving farewell to their new allies.

That was some fantastic negotiating you did back there, Olav signed to Selene as the village faded into the horizon.

Selene grinned. *And I did it without saying a single word.*

Or pulling a knife on anyone, Edric added.

I'm not ruling it out, she signed. *Let's see how the next stop goes.*

Selene, Edric, and Olav repeated this routine four more times before the lodestone finally brought them to the hidden land. They made shore in blazing deserts, lush jungles, frigid icebergs, and rocky cliffs, refilling their supplies at every stop and putting on the Visiting Royalty act any time the inhabitants posed a threat. One of the villages spoke Latin and one stop had no nearby settlements, but even in places Edric couldn't translate directly, a few well-chosen signs that looked similar to their meanings allowed them to communicate well enough to avoid trouble.

Once Selene confirmed the hidden land would make a suitable new home for the library, they made the rounds again, heading south this time, to be sure they could navigate reliably enough to bring the Librarian's people with them. Olav discovered that the flashes of light transporting them from one stretch of ocean to another followed a pattern. The hidden land was the fifth stop heading north, and sailing south when leaving it would bring them to Cyril's island.

Four months later everything was ready. The Librarian's people constructed a single massive cargo ship and ferried both settlers and books along in batches, with Olav the Waymaster stationed at the front to open the path for them with his legendary lodestone. These journeys went much faster than his initial exploration with Selene and Edric since there was no need to stop at each port along the way. In only a week, the sinking island was empty once more.

Olav named the hidden land Falinnheim, which simply meant "hidden land" in his native tongue. (He never was terribly creative with words, but Olav didn't care—after all, his best friend had enough skill with words for both of them.) As Falinnheim's first leader, Cyril was given the honor of naming the newly constructed capital city. Since he was confident the library had found its permanent home, he decided to name it after its founding location:

Alexandria. That way, he could finish his service as Royal Librarian exactly as he began it, ensuring the Library of Alexandria would welcome all books and all scholars, wherever they might be from and whatever perspectives they contained.

Olav the Waymaster, Edric the Wordy, and Selene the Negotiator traveled the world in search of supplies to build their infant country and new records to add to the library. With Olav to navigate the seas, Edric to communicate with their trading partners, and Selene to intimidate anyone who posed a problem, they made an unstoppable team.

After five more years, Olav finally returned the viking dragon ship to Björnvald. Since it turned out his mother was the only one who had missed him, he invited her to settle in Falinnheim with him.

Edric made a trip back to his home, too. His brother Alfred had become lord of the manor by this time, and he didn't think it would be right to leave his duties behind. But though Alfred never did move to Falinnheim, Olav helped Edric bring his entire family over to Falinnheim for a visit twice a year. And when Alfred married and had children of his own, he knew exactly what to do about his younger children: they would take on apprenticeships with their Uncle Edric, who could instruct them equally well in languages and foreign diplomacy as he could in blacksmithing. They had no need to worry about inheriting a family manor. They'd make homes of their own in

Falinnheim, which had land and opportunity to spare.

Cyril the Librarian lived to the distinguished age of one hundred and two. Selene was a bit intimidated to take his place leading Falinnheim, but by that time she'd had so much practice pretending to be in charge that she decided doing it for real couldn't be so terrible. At least, not with her best friends by her side. She made Edric an offer to serve as Falinnheim's official translator and ambassador and made Olav an offer of marriage.

Both were delighted to accept.

CHAPTER 12
BACK TO THE LIBRARY

Tuesday closed *The Book of the Founders* and dropped it in her lap. There were hundreds of pages yet to go, but her brain was brimming with too many new revelations to risk overloading it with more just yet. An unspoken understanding hung in the air as Tuesday, Zed, and Bastian sat in silence, digesting what they'd read. Nyx, who had long since finished her dinner, wandered over and laid her head in Bastian's lap.

"So Falinnheim really was connected to the rest of the world," Zed commented at last. "It's not just that transporters used to be allowed—they're the whole reason Falinnheim got started in the first place."

"Well, sort of," Tuesday corrected him. "I mean, the fancy compass transporters like Scrimbley's must have been invented later. But Olav's lodestone sounds like it did the same job."

"This also explains why Mom's whole family was obsessed with ravens. Olav thought they were some sort of magical helper animals."

"Yeah, what a dumb idea," Bastian teased, petting Nyx. "Who ever heard of animals with unexplained powers hanging out with Falinnheim's leader?"

Zed laughed. "Okay, good point. Maybe getting help from the ravens wasn't just in Olav's imagination after all."

"But Olav wasn't even Falinnheim's leader," Tuesday pointed out. "Selene was."

"Selene was Falinnheim's *second* leader," said Bastian. "Who would have guessed Falinnheim's founding ruler was a librarian? If Uncle Gil knew, he'd never stop going on about it."

"Uh, pretty sure he *does* know," said Zed. "The book was hidden in his library, right behind the shelf for his favorite author. There's no way he hasn't noticed one of Shakespeare's books is stuck to the shelf."

"Maybe he noticed the book, but he doesn't know how to use it," Bastian suggested. "I mean, *we* don't really understand how it works, either. I wonder why I could pick it up, but you and Tuesday couldn't?"

Tuesday was done wondering. It was time to get some answers. "I want another look at that secret room. Gilford's trapped in a meeting right now. We might never get a better chance to figure out how the Shakespeare key works without him spying on us."

Zed wasn't sure he'd call his tutor's attention "spying", exactly—more like "basic supervision" and "actually doing his job"—but Tuesday had a point. They might not get an opportunity like this again. So he took *The Book of the Founders* from Tuesday, shelved it on the crates with the rest of Bastian's collection, and held the door open as Bastian, Nyx, and Tuesday filed out of the bunker.

Tuesday checked the clock stationed across from Gilford's empty desk as they tiptoed into the library. Good! They hadn't even been gone an hour yet. She had no idea what was so important about this meeting her mother had called, but if Gilford was invited to speak his mind, that could take all night. Plenty of time to work in a bit more sleuthing before the adults came back.

Zed grabbed the magnifying glass from the top of Gilford's desk as they filed past.

"Good thinking," Bastian whispered.

The S shelf looked exactly as they'd left it. Tuesday and Zed tried everything they could think of to move *Love's Labour's Lost,* but the book refused to budge. Then, exactly as before, Bastian picked it up without the slightest bit of effort.

The shelf swung backward on hidden hinges into the darkened closet, but Tuesday didn't go inside just yet. She wanted a closer look at the key book first. Bastian passed it over to her, and Zed volunteered the magnifying glass. All three of them huddled close and craned their necks for a better view as Tuesday raised and lowered the glass, trying to bring the book's bottom edge into focus.

"You're using it all wrong," said Bastian, taking the magnifying glass back from Tuesday. "You're supposed to put the glass up to your eye, and then lean toward the book until it's in focus. You'll never see all the tiny details doing it the other way around."

Bastian bent forward with the glass. Tuesday and Zed nearly clonked heads as they tried to lean in too, but Bastian's head blocked their view.

"I don't see anything so far," he said, squinting through the glass as Tuesday slowly rotated the closed book for him to examine from different angles. He shuffled over to peer into the empty space on the shelf, while Zed and Tuesday flipped through the book's pages to check for anything unusual inside it.

They were all so busy searching for clues that they didn't even notice they weren't alone.

"Looking for a bit of light reading?"

Tuesday, Zed, and Bastian looked up in horror as Gilford emerged around the neighboring row of shelves. They didn't even have time to sputter excuses. They just stood there, mouths frozen open in shock, as he strolled forward and took the book from Tuesday.

"As pleased as I am to see my students finally taking an interest in Shakespeare, I can't say I'd recommend this particular play as a starting point. His early work wasn't quite as resonant as some of the later plays. But perhaps literary analysis wasn't the type of book investigation you had in mind?"

"How—?" Tuesday started, but Gilford cut her off before she could finish the question.

"I've known you three were up to something all afternoon. Partly because you're not as stealthy as you think you are," he explained, gesturing to the open shelf door. "You put the books back in mostly alphabetical order, but I could hardly fail to notice you'd switched *King John* and *King Lear*. Partly, because I'm not as stupid as you think I am—clearly, you had some reason to send me on today's wild dodo hunt. Or a wild *flea* hunt, rather. But mostly, what gave you away was just now, when I left my meeting to retrieve some legal precedent notes from the library's law book section, and the Regent's beast trotted right up to greet me."

As though she knew Gilford was talking about her, Nyx chose that moment to bound around the corner, tongue hanging out, looking absolutely delighted. She slid her front legs forward in a playful bow, her tail wagging furiously.

"I see you managed to open the archive room," he added with a nod at the open door. "I must say, I'm a bit surprised the key worked for you. But then, I've never had anyone else to try it on. I really should take an apprentice one of these days."

"How—?" Tuesday started for the second time. But again, Gilford cut her off.

"Slipsteel," he explained, holding up the key book to show them the bottom edge. "Of course you can't see it—the steelsmith did an excellent job calibrating the color matching. But there's a thin layer of slipsteel embedded in both the book cover and that section of the shelf. In theory, I'm the only person who can separate this book from its place on the shelf, which releases the door lock. But…" He shrugged. "I suppose theories are meant to be tested."

Zed smacked his forehead. Of course! Why hadn't he thought of slipsteel? The fact that Gilford's great-nephew succeeded where he and Tuesday had failed should have been a dead giveaway. The slipsteel must be tuned to respond to Gilford's resonance… and apparently Bastian's resonance was just close enough to fool it. Zed had managed the same thing on his father's slipsteel sword only a few weeks ago. Only that time, he had been trying to change the sword's shape, which admittedly hadn't gone very well. Convincing two matching pieces of slipsteel to let go of each other must be much simpler—so simple Bastian could pull it off without even knowing the slipsteel was there. It was like interrupting the power to an electromagnet.

Zed was so fascinated by this new development that he completely forgot he was supposed to be in trouble. "Is the door lock made of slipsteel too?" he asked.

"No need," Gilford answered. "When the key book is

in place, it holds down a lock button under the shelf. When the book is removed, the button lifts. It's a straightforward mechanical solution."

All the unexpected calmness was more than Tuesday could bear. "Who cares how the door works! Aren't you mad that we snuck in?"

"Not especially," Gilford answered.

Tuesday's frustration exploded. "Then why go to all the trouble of hiding your dumb secret room in the first place?"

"Well of course I had to hide the archive," said Gilford. "Don't be ridiculous. I couldn't leave such important artifacts just sitting out in the open. But who said I was hiding them from *you*?"

"But—"

"Look, I have to get back to the meeting. Your mother is waiting on those legal case files, and once the council reads through them, we'll be debating solutions all night. Why don't we make the archive the subject of tomorrow's study? Then we'll have all the time we need to discuss it."

Gilford returned *Love's Labour's Lost* to its place on the shelf. The bookcase door swung shut. The door lock clicked. And the librarian walked away, his long robes swishing grandly behind him as he strode out of the library.

"Weird," was all Bastian had to say.

"At least we're not in trouble?" Zed offered.

Tuesday scowled. "I can't believe he's making us wait until tomorrow to explain everything."

"I must be hearing things," Zed teased. "For a second there, it almost sounded like you're *excited* to go to class."

CHAPTER 13
TEA TIME WITH GILFORD

"All right, spill it," Tuesday demanded when they gathered in the library after breakfast the next morning. Gilford had strolled in seven minutes late, still clutching a mug of that odd color-changing tea Tuesday had tried on her first visit to the palace. Her stomach did a funny jolt when she noticed the bright purple liquid slowly shifting to a rich magenta as Gilford stirred a sugar cube into the steaming mug. The first time Tuesday had seen this strange drink, it was Tyrren doing the stirring and sipping. And between sips, the dictator had plenty of time to insult his servants, mock his decades' worth of victims, threaten her life, and attempt to spread slanderous lies about her parents.

She shoved the unpleasant sensation to the back of her mind. *Focus, Tuesday! There's a mystery to solve.*

If the dark creases under Gilford's eyes were any

indication, last night's meeting had gone very late indeed. Come to think of it, everyone had looked a bit sluggish at breakfast this morning. Even Obaachan, who despite being the oldest person in the entire palace (or—who knows?—maybe the oldest person in all of Falinnheim) usually had more enthusiasm for her job than the rest of the family combined.

"Better not spill it," Bastian joked, "or the cleaning crew will give you a good telling-off. Besides, I thought you didn't allow food in the library."

"I don't allow animals in the library either," Gilford said, shooting an annoyed glance at Nyx, "and yet here we are. Besides, I only said I don't allow *you* to have food in the library. I think I'm old enough to take responsibility for my own messes."

"You can say that again," Bastian mumbled.

"I meant spill the *information*," Tuesday explained, exasperated. "You promised to tell us about the hidden archive and *The Book of the Founders.*"

Gilford raised an eyebrow at her over the top of his mug. "Who said anything about *The Book of the Founders?*"

Tuesday's ears burned as she realized her mistake. Who was spilling secrets now? "Yeah, well… who told you about the other Earth?" she demanded. "Because it certainly wasn't my mother."

"Fair enough." Gilford set his mug down on the study table and took a seat across from his students. "I think it's high time we were all a bit more transparent with each other. Time to lay out all the cards, so to speak."

"You first," said Tuesday skeptically.

Gilford chuckled. "As you wish. But I think once I've explained, you'll understand why I had to keep some secrets from you. And your mother.

"In a way, it all started with the compasses," he said. "Centuries ago, the Moderator and regents decided that travel between Falinnheim and outside lands was too risky to continue. But they also knew that banning something is the surest way to create a demand for it, and they had no desire to devote all their law enforcement efforts to chasing after rogue travel agents. What they really needed was to make people forget there was any place beyond Falinnheim to travel to. So they sent a proclamation through every city and village announcing the creation of a historical preservation society. The regents asked for book donations—anything that detailed the history of families' immigration to Falinnheim, the languages they spoke, or the lands they had come from would be collected and preserved in the royal archives. They even set up a bounty, paying two Hours for every book the historical society accepted. The citizens considered it an honor to have their ancestors memorialized in a royal collection, and the money didn't hurt either. So on the day the book bounty took effect, people lined up in village squares all across Falinnheim to have their records inspected, and were delighted each time the historians proclaimed one worthy of inclusion.

"No one realized the regents were creating a private collection. Once the records entered the palace library, they never left, and the royal archives are not open to visitors. In the first few years, people asked now and then about the books they'd donated. The palace's answer was always the same: the archive was not yet ready for display. As the decades crawled on, the citizens of Falinnheim forgot all about it. The village elders who still spoke the old languages and remembered the old stories began to die off. Younger generations never learned the history of their ancestors and homelands because they couldn't access the books that mentioned them.

"Once everyone forgot about the rest of the world, it was simple enough to round up the remaining transporter compasses, because few people understood what they were used for in the first place. The Regents Council and the royal scholars still had access to the archives, so they passed the knowledge down among their ranks, teachers entrusting their apprentices with carefully guarded secrets. But for the rest of Falinnheim, the origins of our entire world were just… forgotten."

Gilford finished his tale and returned his attention to his mug, which Zed took as a signal: now it was the kids' turn to show their hand. He explained that they'd gotten suspicious about Gilford's knowledge of the other Earth and went looking for answers, only to discover the key book on the Shakespeare shelf.

"Very sensible," said Gilford with a nod of approval. "You wanted answers, so you turned to the library."

"And then Bastian accidentally opened the archive room," Zed continued, "and we only saw one book that was in English, so we started reading it. And… well, that's it, I guess." He'd been careful not to mention the bunker or any of Bastian's hidden "family heirlooms." The story was true enough without them, and Zed figured those weren't his secrets to share.

"How far have you read?" Gilford asked.

"Only the first few chapters—to the end of the Three Founders' story."

Gilford took another sip. "Sounds like you have a lot more reading to catch up on, then."

"Wait, that's *it*?" Tuesday spluttered. "We break into a collection Falinnheim's leaders have been keeping secret for centuries, and we're not even in trouble?"

Gilford chuckled. "Do you want to be in trouble? I could assign you some extra homework as a punishment, if you like. How about… reading the entire *Book of the Founders*?"

Tuesday was too busy groaning and flopping face-first into her folded arms to argue with him.

"I thought we *wanted* answers," Bastian told her with a frown. "I mean, I get that it's a long book, but reading through it was your idea in the first place. What's the problem?"

"The problem is that Gilford's telling her to do it," Zed informed him. "She was only excited about reading *The Book of the Founders* when she thought it wasn't allowed."

"Yeah, well, that was before I realized it was just more history homework," Tuesday grumbled.

"Listen," Gilford said, "I understand this is confusing. Under normal circumstances, you and Zed would have to wait until you grew up and joined the Regents Council to even know about the book, let alone read it. There are very strict laws governing the secrets Royal Librarians protect—who I'm allowed to share that information with, and when. But since you grew up outside of Falinnheim, it's a little late to insist you can't read the book that proves places outside Falinnheim exist—you already know that. And technically, I didn't *give* the book to you, so it's not like I'm breaking any laws. I'm just not taking it back from you right away."

"What about Bastian?" asked Zed.

"The law only specifies when the Royal Librarian should give new regents access to the book. Unlike the two of you, Bastian won't ever be a regent, so the law doesn't apply. A convenient little loophole, if I do say so myself."

"Who said I was planning to join the Regents Council?" Tuesday snapped. "I never agreed to that."

Gilford gave her a strange look. He held it for a moment, as though deciding whether to argue with her, but finally shrugged and took another sip of his tea. "I'm afraid you'll have to take that one up with your mother."

"Oh, don't worry," Tuesday grumbled, scowling. "I plan to."

Zed didn't scowl, and he didn't argue. But he had to admit this revelation caught him off guard. He'd spent his entire stay at the Resistance base mulling over what apprenticeship he might choose when he turned fifteen. It had never occurred to him that the choice had already been made for him. Which seemed pretty stupid, now that Gilford pointed it out. The entire palace had spent weeks knee-deep in preparations for his mother's coronation. Zed knew he was supposed to attend the ceremony, of course. He understood that Mom's new duties meant the entire family would be staying in Falinnheim for a while—and that he didn't have a way to get back to the other Earth, even if he wanted to. He just hadn't realized his entire life had gotten mapped out for him while he wasn't looking.

Zed's swirling thoughts were interrupted when Bastian spoke up. "There's one thing I still don't understand," he told Gilford. "Well, no—there's actually lots of it I still don't understand. Like what in Hades a 'transporter compass' is, for a start… but Zed and Tuesday can fill me in on that later. What I want to know is: if you're supposed to share the hidden archive with new regents, why doesn't Princess Theadora know about it yet? It sounds like she thought you wouldn't know about the other Earth. But if you were the one to show her the archive when she came of age, *she'd* know that *you* know—you know?"

Good question! Tuesday's eyes flicked over to Gilford. She was expecting more of the same carefree excuses, but the librarian didn't say anything right away. He stared silently into his mug for a few seconds, then set it down with a sigh. Tuesday already knew he was running on less sleep than usual, but now, for some reason… Gilford suddenly looked *tired*.

"I suppose I should tell her." Gilford stared into his mug, speaking quietly as though he was really talking himself into a decision, rather than explaining it to his students. It was almost as if he'd forgotten anyone else was in the room.

"When Princess Theadora first returned to the palace, I assumed it didn't matter anymore. I already knew enough about travel outside of Falinnheim to guess where she'd been hiding out all these years, even if I didn't know the specifics. If she was already familiar with the other Earth, then getting her up to speed on the Founders' secrets wasn't terribly urgent. I intended to wait until after the coronation. But that's just an excuse, really. I've been putting it off."

"Why?" asked Bastian.

Gilford finally looked up. He locked eyes with Zed, then Tuesday. "Has your mother ever told you how she got to the other Earth?"

"Not… exactly," Zed answered. "I mean, I assume Scrimbley had something to do with it, and she said Dad and Nyx came with her, but—"

"Why?" Tuesday interrupted. "Do *you* know?"

"No," said Gilford. "I have no idea. What I do know is the reason I didn't tell her about the archive."

"Which *is*?" Bastian pressed impatiently.

Gilford sighed again and picked up his mug. He took a long, slow sip before he answered. "I never got the chance. Princess Theadora was scheduled to be inducted into the Regents Council on her twentieth birthday. But that morning, Tyrren's forces attacked the palace."

CHAPTER 14
THE STORY SWAP

"Yikes."

Bastian's comment pretty much summed things up for everyone.

"Yikes, indeed," said Gilford grimly.

"You…" Zed hesitated, but finally spit it out. "You were here, weren't you? You were in the palace during the attack?"

Gilford nodded, still staring into his mug. "I didn't see anything. The soldiers were careful to strike when the regents were getting ready for your mother's accession ceremony, so they were all in separate rooms. Then the soldiers rounded up the palace staff and locked us in the banquet hall, pretending they were protecting us from outside invaders. In reality, they needed that time to cover their tracks and make sure all the conspirators had their stories straight. The years that followed of working under Tyrren's thumb were no picnic either. But every time I think about that day—" He shook his head. "I *don't* think about it," he finished. "I can't."

"So you've been avoiding talking to the Princess about the archive because it should have been connected to the Regents Council ceremony," Bastian concluded.

"Wait a minute," Tuesday interrupted. "So what you're saying is—my mother isn't actually an official regent?"

Gilford looked up sharply. "That information stays here," he ordered. "It's just a technicality. Your mother is the only surviving member of the royal family. Falinnheim's leadership clearly belongs with her. The Moderator's accession speech is just a tradition. The fact that he never got a chance to give that speech doesn't change anything."

But Tuesday wasn't listening anymore. Of all the secrets Gilford had shared this morning, this was suddenly the only revelation that mattered. "It's all made up," Tuesday whispered to herself. "We don't actually have to go through with it."

"*It?*" Zed interrupted. "What? You mean Mom's coronation?"

Tuesday didn't answer him. She was too busy plotting. Gilford hastily changed the subject.

"Do you have any questions about what you've read so far?" he asked, forcing a smile. "When I first read the Founders' stories, I had to do a lot of background research to understand all the context. Maps, languages, biographies…"

Zed shrugged. "I don't know about Bastian, but I think Tuesday and I are up to speed. I mean, we're obviously not experts or anything, but at least we've heard of vikings and Alexander the Great and the Library of Alexandria."

"Wait," said Bastian, "I thought all of this was supposed to be a big secret. You're telling me everyone from the other Earth knows about it already?"

"They don't know anything about Falinnheim, but some of the other stuff—sure. What happened to the Library of Alexandria is supposed to be this huge mystery. No one has heard of Olav specifically, but vikings in general are pretty common. I mean, they don't have *actual* vikings anymore, but just the idea of them, I guess. Like, people might dress up as a viking for Halloween, or make a viking the mascot of their football team or something."

"Oh," said Bastian. "Good. Quick question: what's football? Also… you might need to explain Halloween."

Tuesday rolled her eyes. "Why don't we just explain the entire history of the world, while we're at it?"

"That would actually be super helpful," Bastian agreed.

Zed laughed. "It's like each world only has their half of the same stories. The only reason Tuesday and I understand both parts is because we've lived in both places."

"It's a shame you're the only two people in Falinnheim who have that perspective," said Gilford. "Even your parents didn't grow up there—they were just visiting. No one else has been to the other Earth in centuries."

Zed stole a glance at Bastian, who warned him with a subtle head shake. Zed understood. They both knew

Gilford was wrong about that. But Bastian wasn't ready to talk about his collection from the old trunk.

Tuesday let out a bitter laugh. "The *real* shame is that everyone in Falinnheim is being lied to. They have no idea their whole world was an accident. They only live here at all because two guys in a stolen boat got lost."

"I mean, technically that's not true for everyone," Gilford argued. "If anything, it would be more accurate to say that two guys in a stolen boat are the reason *you* ended up here. Olav is your distant ancestor, you know. That's why your mother was set to become a regent in the first place: because she's a direct descendant of the royal line started by Olav and Selene. But not everyone's ancestors came in that first migration with Cyril the Librarian. Plenty of other groups moved to Falinnheim later."

Zed had a sudden realization, like two pieces of a puzzle suddenly clicked together in his mind. He turned to Tuesday. "Remember when we spent Hanukkah with Captain Solomon, and he told the story of his ancestors starting a resistance movement?"

Tuesday rolled her eyes. "As if I could forget! We spent that whole week running around trying not to get kidnapped. Having a Hanukkah party to look forward to every night was the only thing that kept us from being miserable."

Zed suppressed a grim smile. They had, in fact, gotten kidnapped that week—but it was by the Red Hand, who didn't do much of anything *besides* kidnapping people, so he figured that one didn't really count.

"I meant did you remember the *story*," Zed clarified. "Solomon said his people were travelers, looking for somewhere to call home, because they kept getting kicked out of every place they settled. I wonder if that's how they ended up in Falinnheim? Maybe they met a Waymaster and moved everyone here, where people wouldn't be so terrible to them."

"That's exactly right!" said Gilford. "In fact, most of the Founders have similar stories. Emperors, regents, and moderators aren't Falinnheim's only heroes. The whole point of *The Book of the Founders* is to collect the stories of the people and events that shaped the course of our society but might otherwise be forgotten—ordinary people who faced extraordinary circumstances and responded with courage and creativity.

"Falinnheim was mainly settled by people who wanted something different than the rest of the world could offer them. From Olav and Edric, who couldn't fit into the lives their societies had planned for them, to entire groups of people who needed somewhere safe to go, like Cyril the Librarian's people, or your friend Solomon's ancestors. And the book has lots more, too—groups seeking religious freedom, or escaping war, famine, or natural disasters. Olav and the other Waymasters traveled the world inviting people who were in need of a safe place to start a new life. And sometimes, people from Falinnheim ended up going back to explore the lands they left behind. Like Valinora the Grim—she was the first human to befriend one of the Gabriel Hounds terrorizing Falinnheim, and she later toured the other Earth in search of interesting or useful animals to bring back with her. The story of how she rescued the last dodo flock is one of my favorites! And then there's Haruto the Valiant, and Agnes the Steelsmith…"

"Okay, we get it!" said Tuesday. "Lots of cool founders. But now that the book's not a secret anymore, we don't have to waste time reading the entire thing. Can't you summarize the stories for us so we can move on? We'll just memorize a few important names and dates, like any other history class."

Gilford's eyes glittered with excitement. "Nope. The power of these stories isn't just recounting what happened— it's in truly getting to know the people who lived them. There are no shortcuts here, not if you really want to understand. You'll just have to read the book for yourself."

Tuesday sighed. "I was afraid you'd say that."

———

Everything.

At last, it was time to tell everything.

No more picking out the relevant parts of the story or skipping over groundwork that would need too much explaining. No half truths, no simplifications, no glazing over the complicated bits or holding back secrets. Tuesday, Zed, and Bastian retreated to the bunker with Nyx and shared every last detail of their stories.

Bastian told all about his family—how his mother had applied for a transfer from her local village council position to the palace's liaison office so her uncle Gilford could be Bastian's tutor; how his mother and stepfather had met by coincidence in the staff dining hall, then started looking for excuses to run into each other on purpose. He told about weekend visits to his grandfather's spice farm, including the time he discovered a newly hatched lizard among the pepper berries and smuggled it back home to the palace conservatory. He spared no detail in the thrilling adventure of discovering each of the palace's secret passages, and how the laundress had taught him to disappear into the nearest one any time they spotted Tyrren stalking through the corridors. The discovery of the bunker soon followed, which inspired a habit of keeping an eye out for anything overlooked or forgotten. Threadbare cushions, chipped teacups—all the unloved things adults discarded as garbage, Bastian squirreled away to furnish the bunker. His best find, of course, came from his great-grandmother's trunk. And once he "liberated" the Other Earth souvenirs, he had even more reasons to duck into the bunker for hours at a time, studying his new collection while avoiding Tyrren's eye. He quickly became so skilled at disappearing, he admitted, that he even began to dream about it. He recounted a recurring nightmare where the palace walls literally swallowed him up. "I've never told anyone about that," Bastian concluded with a sheepish grin. "Not even my parents. It sounds like a stupid thing to be worried about, talking about it now. But nightmares feel so real at the time, you know?"

When Bastian ran out of stories, they switched. He listened intently as Tuesday and Zed tag-teamed their explanations, starting with what little they knew about their parents' escape to the other Earth and filling in all they'd learned about the founding of the Resistance. They recounted their earliest childhood memories, including Tuesday's growing suspicions about her parents and all the subtle ways they seemed out of place. Bastian cut in with questions now and then, but mostly he listened, scratching Nyx's ears absentmindedly while absorbing tales of soldiers brandishing slipsteel battling a flaming Gabriel Hound, mysterious rhyming clues, and a secret base hidden behind a waterfall. There were spies and smugglers, holograms and hoversleds, crystal balls and compasses, robot stampedes and mobs of ravens.

It took the rest of the morning, but when the tales came to an end, at last all the secrets had been dragged out into the light. Tuesday, Zed, and Bastian might not be ready to share these things with *everyone*, but it was a relief to talk to *someone*. They all agreed that no matter how private or heavy they seemed at the beginning, the tales felt lighter when they were shared. Now no one had to carry their stories alone.

"I guess it's time we got back to our assignment," Bastian

said when the stories were spent. He picked up *The Book of the Founders* and searched its pages for the next chapter.

"And here I thought you were a rebel," Tuesday teased, elbowing him lightly in the ribs. "At this rate, you might have to stop *pretending* to be the teacher's pet and admit you actually *are*."

"Hey, you were all for it when you thought Gilford didn't want you to read the book. It's not my fault you don't know how to enjoy anything unless it's forbidden."

Tuesday laughed and nodded toward the bookshelf crates. "That's pretty bold talk, coming from a guy running an entire secret library of illegal books."

"And you started it right under the nose of a murderous dictator," Zed added. "In his own house!"

"It's your house now," said Bastian. He passed the book to Zed. "So I guess the secret's out."

"Don't ruin it!" Tuesday groaned. "The whole point of telling each other all our secrets is that we *can't* share this stuff with everyone. I mean, it's not like you're about to tell your parents where you disappear to when they think you're studying."

"I mean, technically he always *was* studying in the bunker," Zed pointed out. "They just didn't know *what* he was studying."

"No, Tuesday's right," said Bastian. "I'm not planning to go blabbing about the bunker."

"Me neither," said Zed.

"You got that right," said Tuesday.

The three friends were right in the middle of sealing their pact with a handshake when the door swung open.

CHAPTER 15
INTERRUPTED

Everything happened at once.

Tuesday, Zed, and Bastian stood up.

Nyx bounded toward the door.

Zed hid *The Book of the Founders* behind his back.

Bastian folded forward into a hasty bow.

Tuesday scowled.

Princess Theadora stepped into the bunker and closed the disguised stone door behind her.

"Fancy meeting you here," said the Princess. A wry smile was tugging at the corner of her lips.

"What are you doing here?" Tuesday snapped.

Bastian was too busy staring at his boots to argue with her, but Tuesday was sure she heard him suck in a scandalized breath as the words left her mouth.

"I came to get you for lunch," the Princess answered, ignoring Tuesday's rudeness. "Though I suspect what you really meant to ask was, how did I find you?" She sounded like she was straining to hold back laughter, which made

Tuesday madder than ever.

Tuesday turned a venomous look on Nyx, who had planted herself at Princess Theadora's feet, posing regally while waiting for a pat on the head. "Let me guess," Tuesday said. "We got ratted out by the dog."

"Not exactly." The Princess paused to stroke Nyx's chin. "Although I'll admit I did take a bit of a peek through Nyx's mind. You see, I came to get you from the library, but it was empty. I could tell Nyx was with you, and she seemed relaxed, so I gathered everyone must be safe. But that still didn't tell me where to find you. So I really had no choice but to look through her eyes for a moment and get a glimpse of her surroundings."

Zed was so intrigued to learn exactly how the telepathic connection worked that he almost forgot he'd just gotten busted. He looked around at the bunker's stone walls and floors as though seeing them for the first time. "There are plenty of rooms in the palace that look just like this," he said. "How could you possibly know where we were? Or how to get here from the library?"

Now his mother actually did laugh. It was a long, bubbly, musical cascade, as though her sense of humor had sprung a leak and was spilling out uncontrollably.

This launched Tuesday's scowl into previously unexplored depths. Even Bastian abandoned his manners to look quizzically up at the Princess.

"What's so funny?" Tuesday demanded.

Her mother had to wipe away delighted tears before she could answer. "I'm sorry," she said at last. "It's just,"—a stray giggle escaped—"you children really do forget the world existed before you arrived. This palace is nearly a thousand years old. Dozens of generations grew up inside these walls. Do you really think you're the first ones to get bored and go exploring?"

Zed groaned, which got his mother started laughing all over again. He knew she wasn't making fun of him, really—in fact, it seemed more like she'd been needing a good excuse to let off some steam. They definitely couldn't be in trouble, not when her reaction to catching them red-handed was this gleeful.

"You used to hang out here, too?" Zed guessed.

His mother nodded. "I was the youngest of five siblings, you know—the youngest by quite a bit. By the time I was eight years old all the rest of the family had moved on to apprenticeships or joined the Regents Council. So I had a lot of spare time on my hands, and I needed to make my own fun. I spent nearly every afternoon in this room, writing plays for my dolls to perform and sculpting imaginary creatures out of modeling clay."

She paused to look around, taking in the mountain of floor cushions and the umbrellas dotting the ceiling. "I like how you've decorated. I had a few streamers tacked up— just some colorful fabric scraps knotted together, really— but nothing this elaborate." She strolled over to the crates and looked through the contents, which made Bastian suck in another panicked breath. But she didn't comment about any of it, even after she bent down to read the gilded titles running along the spines of each and every book.

Well, not *every* book. Zed turned slowly as his mother circled the room, adjusting to face her so she wouldn't catch a glimpse of the book he had clutched behind his back.

"I must say I managed to keep it a bit cleaner, though," the Princess continued with a grimace. She gestured at the corner next to the floor pillows, where a collection of dirty dishes was piling up.

"Sorry, Mom," said Zed with a bashful grin. "We'll return those to the kitchen soon, I promise."

"Don't put it off too long," she warned, "or you'll start attracting mice. Well—time to get a move on. Your lunch is getting cold." She opened the disguised door and extended her arm toward the hidden passage beyond it.

Nyx loped smoothly over the threshold's stone blocks and turned, waiting for Princess Theadora to follow. Bastian repeated the Princess's gesture, inviting Zed and Tuesday to go before him. The three kids exchanged subtle fist bumps as they lined up to file through the opening. They couldn't say anything, but there was no need—they were all thinking the same thing. Yet again, they'd gotten busted right in the middle of sneaking around, and somehow managed to avoid punishment.

"Oh!" Princess Theadora interrupted. "I almost forgot."

Tuesday froze with one leg over the threshold as her mother turned back to address them. She hastily rigged up her most compliant smile. "Yes?"

Her mother smiled too. She tilted her head to look around Tuesday, locking eyes with Zed instead, and stuck out her hand. "I'll take that back now."

Zed opened and closed his mouth in silent argument. Since he seemed to have forgotten how words worked, Tuesday answered for him. "Take what back?" she asked innocently.

"Whatever it is you've been hiding this whole time." The Princess waggled the fingertips of her outstretched hand, her empty, upturned palm waiting expectantly.

"It's… just homework," Zed tried to explain, but his guilty expression wasn't any more convincing than his wilting attempt at an excuse.

"Nice try, mister. You really expect me to believe you'd go to so much trouble to keep your *homework* a secret?"

"But it really *is* homework!" Tuesday protested as Zed plopped the book into his mother's palm. "Ask Gilford—he'll tell you."

Princess Theadora let out a patient chuckle. "Tuesday June," she said, shaking her head. (Tuesday winced and flicked a furtive, mortified glance back at Bastian.) "Since when are you so anxious to get your schoolwork done on time? Now I really have heard everything."

Nyx's toenails clicked against the echoing stone floors as she led the way down the secret passage and back through the portrait hole. The Princess strode victoriously along behind her. But the tail end of the procession was notably less cheerful.

"At least now you don't have to do all that history reading," Zed whispered glumly to Tuesday. "That's what you wanted, right?"

Tuesday responded with an indistinct sulking noise.

"Not anymore," Bastian answered for her. "Tuesday only wants what she can't have."

———

Two days passed before anyone brought up *The Book of the Founders* again. Tuesday wasn't certain whether Gilford knew Mom had confiscated it, but she suspected not. The librarian seemed determined to avoid revisiting the trauma of the day he should have given it to the Princess in the first place, so he wasn't likely to open up that conversation himself. As Regent, Mom didn't need anyone's permission to access classified information, so it's not like she had any responsibility to give it back to Gilford.

Tuesday was still mad at both of them: Gilford for making her read the book, and her mother for preventing her from reading it. Plus, Tuesday was still sulking about Mom ruining the secrecy of the bunker, so she wasn't exactly in a chatty mood. Which is why she decided to make Zed do the negotiating for her.

The Furst family had an entire wing of the palace to themselves. The whole seventh floor was reserved for residence suites, which kept living areas separate from the support staff workspaces, government offices, and public entertaining rooms like the portrait gallery and banquet hall. But even if an intruder (or more likely, a new government employee or a lost visitor) managed to access the seventh floor, they wouldn't make it any further. The hallway dead-ended at a pentagon-shaped landing featuring five identical sets of heavy oak doors, which separated the different residence wings. All locked, naturally. Captain Beren had made a lot of security upgrades since he took over the Royal Guard.

The Regents Wing used to be further divided so the different branches of the Moderator's extended family could each have their own space. But there was no need for that anymore, since Princess Theadora was the only regent left. Which is why there was enough space for Tuesday's parents to have their own private living room and study attached to their bedroom.

Tuesday peeked around the doorway to her parents' lounge. Her mother was stretched out on a mustard-yellow sofa, her long wavy hair sprawled across an embroidered pillow, propping up her chin with one hand as she slowly turned the pages of the massive blue book in front of her.

That massive blue book.

"She's right there," Tuesday whispered to Zed. "Just go ask her."

"Why don't *you* ask her?" he hissed.

"You want the book back, or not?"

"Sure, but why do *I* have to be the one to—"

Nyx broke the stalemate by trotting out from their hiding place and flopping down on the antique rug in front of the sofa, scootching her back against the carved sofa legs so she'd be in easy petting reach. The Princess dangled one arm down and gave Nyx a distracted scruff ruffling, but she didn't look away from her reading.

Tuesday nudged Zed out from their hiding place. "Go on," she mouthed silently.

Zed glared at his sister, but he knew there was no point arguing with her. She was going to get her way eventually. Might as well get it over with.

He stood and cleared his throat to announce his presence as he strolled into the lounge. "Hey, Mom," he said casually. "Enjoying your book?"

His mother made a brief hum of agreement and turned another page.

"So, Tuesday and I were wondering—"

An annoyed cough erupted from the hallway.

"—I mean *I* was wondering if maybe we could—"

But Zed never got to finish his question. His mother's eyebrows scrunched together. She flipped back to the previous page and read intensely for a moment, then turned ahead a page and repeated the procedure.

"Everything… okay?" Zed ventured.

His mother finally looked up, beaming. "I know what to

do!" she announced.

———————

As usual, Princess Theadora's first instinct was to call all her advisors into a meeting. And as usual, the proceedings were top-secret, so Tuesday and Zed were *not* invited. It hardly mattered, though. They might be the only members of their family excluded from the meeting, but once it was over, it seemed the entire palace was involved in launching the Princess's plan. It didn't take much eavesdropping in the staff dining hall for Bastian to gather what everyone was up to.

"A bunch of the palace guards got their duty schedules switched around at the last minute," Bastian reported when they met for class the next morning. "The higher-ranking officers all got pulled for a special assignment, so everyone else has to cover their posts. My stepdad got instructions to modify a cargo hoversled with a big metal cover so no one can see what's in it. Obaachan made a long list of supplies for the kitchen stewards and linen maids to gather and pack in crates—food that will keep for a long time, mostly, but also clothes and blankets, dishes, cleaning supplies, tools, and some simple furniture. And my mom said the village liaison office spent all evening trying to track down specialists and deliver them Royal Summons. She didn't know what the summons actually said, but the people they were trying to contact had some interesting similarities. Aside from one psychology professor, they were all technology experts. I think she mentioned a crystal electronics specialist, an inventor, and somebody from Hololab Industries."

"Where have I heard that name?" Zed muttered.

"Hololab?" Bastian asked. "I mean, I know you two don't get out much anymore, but it would be weird if you *hadn't* heard of them. Hololab is the richest tech business in all of Falinnheim. They *invented* holograms. I guess there are a few knock-off competitors now, but everyone knows Chatgram and Projetonics holograms aren't near as good—they get all glitchy." He laughed. "I remember one summer I went to visit my grandpa in North Tarlington. The local ice cream shop got a Projetonics hologram to take orders so the employees wouldn't have to do anything except scoop. But no matter what you asked the hologram for, he always insisted you needed to try the Turnip Mint Chip. The shop lost so much business, it was only a week before they threw the projector in the dumpster and went back to hiring real people."

"Now I remember!" said Zed. "When we needed Scrimbley's help to break into the Resistance base. He said somebody from Hololab Industries programmed the holograms in Persepolis with Mom's clues when we first arrived in Falinnheim. He'd learned from the technician how to do it, so he knew how to hack into the base's hologram system."

Tuesday nodded sagely. "Whatever Mom's up to, it makes

sense she'd want the best in the business to help her out. The boss at Hololab will do the job right. Not like Scrimbley, slapping a cheap solution together for bribe money."

"That's the weird part," said Bastian. "Well—two weird things, actually. My mom thought she'd be tracking down the owner of Hololab Industries, or at least some executive in the installation division, but it was someone else. That's why she mentioned it at all. She couldn't get over how strange it was that the Princess didn't want the boss. The summons was for an employee—just a regular service technician. I mean, not just *any* technician; she asked for one particular guy by name. But he's not the boss of anything."

"Yeah, that is strange," Zed agreed.

"What was the second weird thing?" Tuesday asked.

"I'd forgotten until you mentioned his name just now," said Bastian. "Scrimbley—that smuggler you told me about? He was on the list, too."

Tuesday rolled her eyes. "Of course he is. Mom's got some weird obsession with that weasel."

"Hey, he's actually come in pretty handy," Zed argued. "You may not like Scrimbley, but he accomplished all the stuff Mom, Baba, or Captain Solomon ever asked him for. He didn't even get paid to help out at the Solstice parade— he genuinely wanted Mom to succeed. And Nyx likes him," he added, reaching down to rub the dog's ears, "so there's that. She's always been a good judge of character."

"Oh, Scrimbley's a character, all right," said Tuesday. "But I wouldn't jump straight to *good*."

The discussion broke up when Gilford arrived to start the day's lessons. Tuesday, Zed, and Bastian bombarded him with questions, but as usual, he kept all the juiciest details to himself. They tried everything from trick questions to bribery, but all they managed to get out of him was that yes, he had been summoned to the Princess's meeting. No, he couldn't talk about it. Yes, *The Book of the Founders* had been a huge help, thanks for asking. Time for mathematics.

At lunchtime, Baba appeared with a tray of sandwiches, which finally convinced Gilford to stop droning on about inverse fractions. He reluctantly agreed to a half-hour lunch break. "But no wandering off," he warned, fixing each of his students with a stern stare. "We're diving right back into the distributive property when I get back."

"Typical," said Tuesday as she watched Gilford leave. "First we're not supposed to eat in the library, and now we're not allowed to take our food *out* of the library. I wish he'd make up his mind."

"Trust me, you don't want to be in the dining room anyway," said Baba as she settled in at the study table and started passing around sandwich triangles.

"Why not?" asked Bastian.

"There are a lot of visiting consultants working on your mother's… *plan*. She got stuck with hosting duties. Let's just say it's a bit more crowded in there than usual. And a lot less private."

Tuesday nearly spit out her grilled cheese. "Wait, Mom summoned everyone *here*? To the palace?"

"Which part of Royal Summons are you unclear on?" Zed asked. "They got *summoned*. Which means 'show up or else.' Where did you think they'd be meeting?"

"But… that means *he's* here."

Tuesday didn't have to explain who "he" was. Baba offered her a grim smile. "Why do you think I'm hiding out up here?"

"What's Mom want with him anyway?" Zed asked. But he knew it was a pointless question. If they couldn't persuade Gilford to part with secrets, they weren't likely to make any better progress pestering a legendary spy. Baba could keep her lips sealed until dodos learned to fly.

Bastian looked from the General to Tuesday, trying to read into their irritated grimaces. "Are we talking about who I think we're talking about? Because I'd actually like to meet him. See if his reputation lives up to all the hype."

"Trust me," said Tuesday, "I wasn't exaggerating. If anything, I sugarcoated it. That guy could pick a soldier's pocket, empty his wallet, then turn around and sell the wallet back to him for twice what it's worth. And somehow, the soldier would still walk away thinking he'd gotten the better end of the deal."

"Do my ears deceive me," called a voice from the doorway, "or did I hear the word *deal*?"

Tuesday didn't even bother looking over her shoulder. She'd know that voice anywhere. She groaned and buried her face in her hands.

"Looks like you got your wish," Zed laughed. He gestured toward the short, scruffy, middle-aged man now sauntering into the library. "Bastian—meet Scrimbley."

CHAPTER 16
THE SMUGGLER'S DILEMMA

"What are you doing here?" Tuesday demanded.

Baba managed to phrase her thoughts slightly more civilly (but only slightly.) She didn't even bother to look up from her plate. "I'm fairly certain Her Highness intended all her guests to stay in the dining room," she said curtly.

"Went looking for a bathroom," said Scrimbley. He stuck his hands in his trouser pockets and gazed around at the endless bookshelves with mild curiosity.

"You failed pretty hard, then," said Tuesday. "Clearly, this isn't one."

"Funny thing about that—technically, the hallways and art collections and suchlike are open to the public. You need an invitation to get inside the palace in the first place, but once you're in, you can go pretty much anyplace that isn't locked up."

"That definitely isn't true," Bastian informed him.

"Ah, my mistake then," said Scrimbley cheerfully. "No one stopped me, though. So in a way, that's their fault. Can't blame a fella for being lost and curious, now can you?"

Tuesday could, and she absolutely would. But for the moment, her disapproval seemed to be the only consequence she could muster. Nyx was too busy scarfing down her bowl of kitchen scraps to even bother looking at the intruder. Fat load of help Mom's "bodyguard" turned out to be.

Still—maybe she could use Scrimbley's casual relationship with rules to her advantage. If he didn't care about trespassing all over the palace, Tuesday reasoned, maybe he didn't take secrecy very seriously either.

"What does my mom want you to do for her?" she asked.

"Same as I does for everyone." Scrimbley plunked himself down at the table next to Zed. "I solves problems."

Now Zed was getting intrigued too. "What problem does my Mom have?"

"I think you know the answer to that," he said cryptically. "Same problem as all of Falinnheim's got."

"What are you talking about?" Tuesday asked. "The only problem that affected everyone in Falinnheim was Tyrren, and he's taken care of."

Scrimbley tapped his nose and winked at her. "Is he, though?"

"Of course," Zed insisted. "He's in jail, isn't he?"

"Ah, but what then?" Scrimbley asked. "Can't keep him in the dungeon forever, can we? What if he breaks out? What if he convinces his old friends with the red gloves to skulk about and run errands for him? That man's as dangerous as a cornered cobra. But you can't have him executed, either—wouldn't look right. People would say the Princess is taking revenge. Say she's disposing of her enemies just the same as he did."

"All right," Tuesday snapped. "What's the answer then, if you're so smart?"

Baba looked up from her plate and fixed Scrimbley with her best You'll Keep Quiet If You Know What's Good For You stare.

Scrimbley must have gotten the message. He gulped hard and began inspecting his dirt-caked fingernails.

"Tyrren did horrible things," Baba said calmly. "His stories are not for children's ears. That's why you weren't called on to testify at his trial. Everyone involved agreed you should never have to deal with him again. That hasn't changed. So this conversation is over now." She turned to Scrimbley. "Which means you have no reason to be here."

Scrimbley stood up, but he didn't leave right away. "The Princess brought me in to work out a solution," he said, wandering around and glancing over the rows of books again, "and that's what I intends to do. She's got half an idea already—just needs help figuring how to pull it off. Said she got a flash of inspiration while reading a book." He laughed. "Don't get much time for reading, myself. Maybe I oughta give it a go sometime." He shot a significant look over at Zed and Tuesday, then strolled out of the library, whistling to himself as he went.

Baba was quick to change the subject, and the others knew better than to argue with her. But there was really no need for discussion. Bastian, Tuesday, and Zed exchanged subtle, silent nods. Scrimbley might not know which book had kicked off the Princess's plan, but they did.

"Speaking of looking for a bathroom," Zed announced, "I think I'll make a stop, too."

"Great idea," said Bastian, getting up. "Wouldn't want to interrupt Uncle Gil's lesson time later."

"You might as well all go," Baba agreed. "But no wasting time—your lessons start back up in ten minutes."

"No problem," said Tuesday with a grin. "Unlike Scrimbley, we know exactly where we're going."

They certainly did. Without a word, Bastian, Zed, and Tuesday hustled up flights of stairs until they reached the seventh-floor landing. Zed pulled his key out of his pocket and unlocked the imposing set of carved wood doors to the royal residence wing.

"Maybe I should wait here," Bastian whispered. "I don't think I'm allowed past the landing."

"Don't be ridiculous," Tuesday scoffed. "I live here. I'm allowed to invite friends over. Besides, where's your sense of adventure? I thought sneaking around the palace was your favorite thing."

"Secret passages are for the staff anyway," he argued. "This is different. If I got caught breaking in somewhere this secure, my parents could lose their jobs."

"Good thing we're not breaking in, then," said Zed, waving the key at Bastian before tucking it back in his pocket.

"I guess…" But Bastian didn't seem convinced. He looked cautiously over his shoulder to make sure they were alone. Which is when he discovered they definitely weren't.

Bastian flinched and made a noise like he'd accidentally swallowed a bee.

Zed and Tuesday whirled around to see what all the fuss was about.

Nyx was standing right behind them.

No one had heard her following them up the stairs, but sneaky silent walking was pretty low on the list of Weird Gabriel Hound Powers, so nobody bothered to comment on it. The bigger issue, as Bastian pointed out, was that if Nyx could see them, there was a chance Princess Theadora could, too.

"Only if she's got a reason to go looking," said Zed. "Which she won't do unless Nyx senses something's wrong. All we have to do is keep Nyx happy, and she'll assume everything is fine. And besides, even if Mom does turn on the telepathy, she can only see whatever Nyx is looking at. There's nothing unusual about us hanging out at home."

They filed through the door and locked it behind them.

Zed got assigned to sit in the front hall and pet Nyx, making sure she faced the door so she couldn't watch the others doing anything suspicious. Meanwhile, Tuesday headed for her parents' study.

As she had hoped, *The Book of the Founders* was waiting on the end table next to the sofa. Her mother had taken it with her to last night's planning meeting, but with the palace now crawling with visitors, it had probably seemed safer to lock it up in the residence wing.

"Better hurry," Bastian warned. "We've only got a few minutes until Uncle Gil comes back and wonders where we are."

Tuesday flipped through the pages until the book fell open to a section near the end, where a green hair ribbon had been left as a bookmark. She assumed this marked the last thing her mother had read before calling the emergency council meeting. There wasn't time to read the entire chapter, but maybe she could skim enough of it to figure out what had gotten Mom's plan rolling.

As her eyes sped over the lines of text, they kept getting caught on capitalized words. These were mostly names of people and places, which didn't really reveal what the story was about, so she quickly abandoned this strategy and turned her full attention to the last page of the chapter.

"Looks like this story is about a volcano," Tuesday reported. "It keeps mentioning eruptions and ash clouds." She turned to Bastian. "*Are* there volcanoes in Falinnhiem?"

"Uncle Gil spent an entire afternoon on geography class just a couple days ago. Weren't you paying attention?"

"I had more important things on my mind," Tuesday huffed. "Like, oh, I don't know… the fact that the library has a secret room hiding centuries' worth of banned books? Just answer the question!"

"I've never heard of a volcano actually erupting," said Bastian, "but this story's probably pretty old. Falinnheim has two separate mountain ranges. I guess some of the mountains might have been volcanoes a long time ago."

"The walkways in the conservatory are paved with black pebbles," Zed called from his post by the door. "I'm pretty sure they're made of lava rock. All those rocks had to come from somewhere."

"A volcanic eruption would be a huge problem," Bastian agreed. "Even if you could avoid the actual lava, the ash cloud would cover everything. Falinnheim may be big, but it's still an island—there would be no way to escape from a disaster that major."

"So what does the story say they did about it?" Zed asked.

Tuesday read through the last paragraph. "Looks like they used a transporter compass. Or maybe it took several compasses? It says the Waymasters transported everyone out of Falinnheim temporarily. They waited for the ash and toxic gasses to settle down, then brought everyone back."

"Everyone?" Bastian asked dubiously. "Transported them where?"

"Doesn't say. Someplace empty—seems like they were basically camping. The book just calls it Elsewhere."

"Time's nearly up!" Zed called. "Let's go. We can come back after school and have more time to read the whole thing."

But Tuesday wasn't willing to take chances. The book was only available at the moment because her mother was too busy shaking hands and passing around fancy finger foods to catch up on her reading. What if she came back for the book when the visitors' reception ended? If they smuggled the book back to the library, Mom would know she and Zed took it—no one outside the family could get into the lounge in the first place. The bunker wasn't safe either—Mom knew about that, too. They couldn't count on the book still being here after school ended. They needed an answer *now.*

Desperate, she flipped through the remaining pages, hoping something useful would leap out at her. And then, to her astonishment, something did.

In most books, the last couple of pages are left blank. Tuesday had never really thought about why this might be, but she knew she had seen it before. It didn't strike her as unusual when she got to the last page and found it empty. She briefly thought about checking the page for invisible ink. (Something to do with lemon juice? Zed would know.) But then she turned the page over for a look at the inside of the book's back cover.

She had no idea what it meant. But there was definitely writing, and it definitely wasn't invisible.

24 / 5 / 4   300 / 13 / 8   172 / 23 / 1

56 / 7 / 7   1 / 1 / 1   42 / 7 / 2

67 / 14 / 9   2 / 15 / 6   88 / 17 / 4

The rest of the book used black machine-printed text, but the collection of numbers was hand-written. The blue ink had started to fade slightly, bleeding yellow around the edges, but the numbers were still clearly legible.

Tuesday sighed and passed the book to Bastian. "Every time we think we've got things figured out, this dumb book throws another mystery at us! There's no way we can crack this code before we go back to class," she grumbled. "At this rate, we'll be lucky if we figure it out before we're Obaachan's age."

But Bastian just smiled. His eyes lit with a triumphant gleam. "Wanna bet?"

CHAPTER 17
THE CIPHER

"Now you're just messing with me," said Tuesday. "You don't know what all those numbers mean."

"No," Bastian admitted, "I don't. But I know how to find out."

Zed wandered over. "What's taking so long?"

"Aren't you supposed to be watching Nyx?" Tuesday retorted.

"I gave her one of Dad's old boots to chew on. She'll be busy for a while."

Tuesday wanted to argue that, distraction or not, Zed was still abandoning his post. But Bastian cut in before she got the chance. "Perfect timing!" he said, pointing at Zed. "Have you got your notebook?"

"Always." Zed dug the notebook and a pencil out of his tunic pocket and handed them over.

Zed watched as Bastian flipped to a blank sheet and copied down the handwritten page of numbers. "Hey, you guys were holding out on me!" Zed said. "Why didn't you

"

tell me you'd found a book cipher?"

"A what?" asked Tuesday.

"It's an old method for sending secret messages," Zed explained. "You find the words you want to use in a book, then use numbers to describe each word's location inside the book." He pointed to the handwritten list on the last page. "See how each group has a set of three numbers? I'm guessing the first one is a page number, the second one says which line on that page, and for the third number you count over that many words on the line. So to find the first word in the message we turn to page twenty-four, count down to the fifth line, and find the fourth word on that line."

"It's a really simple system," Bastian agreed, "but it's *genius*. The sender and the receiver of the message just need identical copies of the same book. When the coded message arrives, you pull out your copy of the book and do a little counting to figure out what it says. If the wrong person intercepts the code, they probably won't know what they're looking at. And even if they do recognize that it's a book cipher, they won't know which book to use as a decoding legend. This means the code is practically unbreakable."

"Perfect," Tuesday grumbled, "just what we need—a code we *can't* break."

"Ah, but that's only if people are sending messages to each other through the mail or something," Bastian reminded her. "This is different."

"How?"

Bastian didn't answer. He just kept scribbling.

"In a way, this message *was* sent to us," Zed added thoughtfully. "But instead of sending the information across distance, it's traveling across time."

"Wait, now we're talking about *time travel?*" Tuesday blurted.

"Not the way you're thinking of," said Bastian. "But Zed is right. Whoever left this code wanted it to be found by the next person to read this book. We have no idea how long ago the code was added, or by who. It could have been decades ago—centuries, even."

It was harder to keep arguing when it was two against one, but Tuesday still wasn't entirely convinced. "How do you know about this, anyway?"

Bastian shrugged. "Sherlock Holmes solved a mystery with a book cipher in it. He had to figure out what book to use for a decoding legend. Turned out to be a really common book—an almanac, I think. The idea was that everyone in London would have access to a copy."

"So… we need to find the most common book in Falinnheim?" Tuesday asked.

"Nope." Zed held up *The Book of the Founders*. "In this case, we need the *rarest* book in Falinnheim. And we just happen to have the only copy."

Zed and Bastian worked together, flipping through the book's pages and counting off lines and words, until they'd translated the entire code and copied the message down in Zed's notebook.

PLANTED INSIDE SILENT BARK THE HEART LEAVES ANOTHER STORY

"Sounds like a riddle," said Tuesday. "I still don't get why you'd hide a code in the exact same book you'd use to translate it. Why not just skip the numbers and write the decoded message?"

"I dunno," said Zed. "Maybe whoever wrote the riddle wanted to make sure only people who had studied all the book's details would find it. Make it harder to understand on purpose, so you'd have to really care about it to find the answer."

That made no sense to Tuesday either—if she wanted to share important information, she'd make it *easier* to understand, not harder—but she decided to let it go, for the moment. They were late for class.

———

The conservatory. That part was obvious. Or at least it seemed obvious to Zed. The riddle had to be leading them to the conservatory. Where else in the palace were things "planted inside"? Of course, the code hadn't said anything about the palace at all… but since they had nowhere else to look, he decided to keep that worry to himself. *The Book of the Founders* was stored in the palace library, after all. He'd just have to trust that whoever wrote the riddle had known that.

Bastian suggested there might be some kind of gargoyle or statue marking the spot. A real animal wouldn't still be there guarding a hiding place after all these years, but a carving of an animal—a dog, maybe—could have a "silent bark."

Tuesday wasn't so sure about that, but the appeal of finding "another story" kept her from criticizing the boys' ideas. Especially if it was a story Mom and Gilford didn't know about. So when Gilford finally released them from class that afternoon, she agreed the conservatory was a decent place to start their treasure hunt. The hard part was figuring out what to do when they got there.

"The gardeners work in here all the time," Bastian pointed out. "Some of the plants are here year-round, but some have to be dug up and replanted every year. What if someone already found whatever the riddle is leading to and moved it? Or didn't know it was important and threw it away?"

"Plus, we have no idea how long ago the book code was written," Zed added. "The entire conservatory could have been remodeled since then."

"Anyone smart enough to leave coded clues probably would have thought that through," said Tuesday. Saying it out loud helped Tuesday convince herself it must be true. She couldn't stand the thought that they might be hundreds of years too late to solve the mystery. "Whatever we're looking for, it has to be hidden someplace it wouldn't get bothered on accident."

Her eyes swept the conservatory. If she had important secrets to protect, where would she hide them? Bastian was right—anything buried might get dug up during weeding or replanting, so that didn't seem likely. The floors were gravel, so there were no loose floorboards or stone blocks to tuck something under. The raised planting beds had stone block walls, though… maybe one of them had a dog carved into it to mark the spot? Bastian's "silent bark" explanation sounded reasonable enough. She started down the gravel path, Nyx trotting along after her, to scan the blocks for further clues.

Twenty minutes later, she found it: the perfect stone planter ledge to flump down on in frustration. "This is impossible!" she complained. "How could the code writer think a few random words from a book would be enough information? We're never going to find it." She leaned back against a tree trunk and closed her eyes.

"Uh… Tuesday?" said Zed. "You might want to move."

"No, don't move!" said Bastian. "Hold verrrry still…"

Tuesday's eyes popped open in alarm. "Why? What's going on?"

Zed pointed at the tree behind her, where a tiny green lizard was squiggling its way down the trunk. "I think Queen Elizardabeth wants to check out your hair."

She jumped up, but too late: Queen Elizardabeth leaped off the tree trunk and landed right on top of Tuesday's head.

"Get it off!" Tuesday squealed. She raised her hands to

brush the lizard away, but then remembered Bastian's pet had a habit of biting. So she froze in place with her fingers fanned out on either side of her ears until Bastian came to her rescue and scooped the lizard onto his shoulder.

Zed laughed so hard he doubled over, clutching his sides. "You should have seen yourself!" he told Tuesday after he caught his breath. "It was like you got halfway through surrendering, then got a sudden urge to do jazz hands. Or like you were a mime testing the walls of an invisible box."

"What's a mime?" Bastian asked. "Also… jazz hands?"

Tuesday started thinking up something scathing to yell at her brother, but then she caught sight of the tree behind her. It was one of those dwarf varieties that had been pruned so it wouldn't get too tall for the conservatory's glass ceiling. Since it couldn't grow upward, it appeared the tree had put all its energy into growing *out*, making the trunk nearly as wide as it was tall. It must have been here for hundreds of years, she thought, to grow a trunk that thick. She glanced up at the foliage. The deep purple leaves were shaped like… hearts.

The heart leaves!

"Silent bark," Tuesday whispered. "The riddle didn't mean a barking animal. It's tree bark."

She ducked under the branches and wound around the back side of the tree. Just as she suspected, there was a large, open knot in the trunk. She wasn't tall enough to see if there was anything in it, but by standing on tiptoe, she could just barely reach inside.

Her fingers brushed rough wood, then smooth metal. "Jackpot!"

Bastian clambered into the planting bed and knelt down next to the tree, propping up one leg so Tuesday could use his knee as a stepstool. She reached into the opening and withdrew their prize: a metal box with a hinged lid on one side and a hook latch on the other. The burnished copper finish had gone green at the corners with age, but it didn't seem too corroded. Hopefully whatever was inside would still be intact.

"Looks like an old jewelry box," Zed informed them when Tuesday and Bastian returned to the open walkway.

Bastian laughed. "I'll be so mad if there's actually treasure inside. Forget gold and jewels. I'm hoping for paper!"

The boys crowded around as Tuesday rotated the latch and creaked open the lid.

There were no jewels, but Bastian was half right. Nestled inside the box's faded blue velvet lining were two identical gold-colored balls, each about the size of a tangerine. But Tuesday ignored them for the moment, shifting them aside to extract the folded sheets of parchment tucked underneath them.

Tuesday set the box down on the ledge so she had both hands free to gingerly unfold the brittle paper. She couldn't be sure the slanted handwriting matched the book cipher, since that had only numbers, but the faded blue ink was definitely the same.

"What's it say?" Zed pressed. "Read it!"

Tuesday cleared her throat and read aloud.

CHAPTER 18
THE CODEWRITER'S LETTER

To whomever finds this letter:

The council has forbidden me to speak about what I have seen, but if I have to keep this knowledge bottled up inside me, I think I might explode. Instead, I am writing it down in the hope that it will someday come to light. Perhaps the people of some future time will be more open to what I have learned.

It's been said that long ago, the people of Falinnheim traveled freely to other lands. We purchased the foreigners' goods, studied their discoveries and inventions, and sometimes invited people of interest to settle with us. But then a great plague swept through a city called London and quickly spread to all the surrounding lands. To protect Falinnheim from the disease, the regents determined that travel to the outside world must end. They granted all the

Waymasters a royal pension and tasked their apprentices to catalog tales of the Founders' voyages, rather than take such voyages themselves. This was intended to be a temporary pause, just until the sickness passed. But fear took hold of the council, who taught that fear to each new regent who joined their ranks, and the tales lost balance in the telling. Soon, the entire council was certain: the outside world was a savage and dangerous place no one would wish to go, with nothing new to contribute to Falinnheim's enlightened society. For the good of the people, it must be erased.

They could not literally erase the world, of course. Falinnheim is merely a pocket in the fabric of reality, as connected to the rest of the Earth as a tunic is to its lining. The best they could do was erase it from memory. If they pretended nothing outside Falinnheim existed, refused to speak or write or read about it, then that would become real, at least in people's minds. So the council gathered anything that didn't align with their Falinnheim-centered narrative and hid it in the royal archive. Some stories from the other Earth were passed off as imaginative fantasies, but anything that described travel to and from Falinnheim was now a government secret.

As generations passed, people forgot that their great-grandparents spoke other languages. They never stopped to reason that a village named New Cairo, or New Stockholm, or New Athens must have been settled by people from the old Cairo or Stockholm or Athens. As far as they knew,

Falinnheim was all that existed, all that had ever been or would ever be. The Regents Council and archive historians knew the truth, since they had access to the hidden records, but it was a closely guarded secret. The rest of Falinnheim was left in the dark.

As an apprentice in the royal archive, I studied many Other Earth artifacts collected over the centuries. When I turned twenty and prepared to graduate from my apprenticeship, my professor granted me a rare honor, usually reserved only for regents: I was permitted to read *The Book of the Founders*. And suddenly, all the ancient maps and journals I'd studied made sense. I realized that though the regents of centuries ago had the best of intentions, their plan to keep people safe had actually kept them captive. They hadn't protected our future. They'd stolen our past.

Armed with this new information, I petitioned the council to send me on a scouting mission to the other Earth. The Waymasters were banned two hundred fifty years ago, I argued. Surely the London plague was over by now. It might be safe to restore the bonds between our worlds.

The council agreed, reluctantly. They still feared the other Earth and assumed its people had achieved nothing that would benefit Falinnheim's "superior" society. But curiosity got the better of them. They allowed me to take a transporter compass from the archive and travel alone, in secret, to spend a single day exploring modern London.

My professor found an old text that described how to use the compass, and an even older atlas that included transporter coordinates for London. After a few trial runs with objects, and then plants, we were confident transporting between worlds was safe.

The first day of the Endeavor season was approaching—what better time to begin a new endeavor? So I made my journey on New Year's Day. My professor set the dials on the compass, and in a flash of light I left the royal archive and appeared in a deserted alley of a massive city.

My clothing was out of place, as I could not predict how fashions might have changed since Falinnheim cut off contact. But I discovered London streets were so busy that no one took any notice of me. It did not appear to be a holiday there. Everyone went about their normal routines, focused on normal problems, and ignored everyone around them. New leaves were budding on the trees, the ground was moist and spongy with overnight rain, and the city was filled with people walking, horses pulling carts, and even mechanical carts that rolled along the pavement without anything to pull them.

I found a pawnbroker's shop where I was able to sell the Hours and Minutes in my pocket (as foreign jewelry—the shopkeeper would not accept the idea that my coins were money) in exchange for local currency. I used this to buy artifacts to take back with me for later study. As I did not have much money to spend, I decided on a street stall selling second-hand books and magazines. The stall did not carry books on history or geography, but I purchased several volumes of stories. This would be a more accurate depiction of their society anyway, I decided. Academic texts are meant to impress; people write what they want others to think. But in fiction, we let slip the truths we don't think to hide.

I was tempted to read the stories then and there, but I knew there would be plenty of time for that when I returned to Falinnheim. Instead, I spent the rest of the day walking the streets and sitting on park benches, studying the people of London and collecting interesting items I found discarded. A day-old newspaper left on the park bench was incredibly instructive, as it mentioned not only the happenings of London, but major news from the rest of the world. Which is where I discovered the war.

Apparently, though I saw no signs of fighting in London, the other Earth is engaged in a "war to end all wars" waged with terrible new weapons: flying machines like giant birds, and swords that fire tiny cannonballs, and clouds of poisonous gas. I could not determine from the newspaper what the conflict is about, only that governments all over the Earth are involved in it. And though the London plague is long over, there are rumors of a new disease sweeping some place called Spain, which they fear will be spread by the traveling soldiers.

At the end of the day, I used the compass to return to

Falinnheim. I stayed up all night reading through the books I'd brought back with me, and in the morning I made my report to the regents.

The Regents Council was horrified to learn that the other Earth was engaged in a war, not just between neighboring kingdoms, but spanning the entire globe. Other Earth technology was impressive, but they appeared to use it only to find more efficient ways to harm each other. The rumor of a worldwide "flu" disease was the final straw.

The fear handed down through generations of regents was entirely justified, they said. The other Earth was too dangerous to risk further contact, even in secret. For the good of Falinnheim, the remaining transport compasses must be destroyed. The Moderator threw the newspaper in the council chamber fireplace. Luckily, I'd left the other books in my bedroom, or the council would have burned those, too.

If the regents had actually studied *The Book of the Founders*, as I have, they would have known how foolish this fearful impulse was. Treating information as a threat, rather than a tool, is exactly what led to the downfall of ancient Alexandria. But history repeats itself, at least until we stop the cycle and learn from our mistakes. Which is why I know exactly what the council will do next.

The regents have already tried banning books. Once they realize that censorship is not enough to control information they disapprove of, they will come for the people studying that information. Just as in the time of Cyril the Librarian, the historians, writers, scientists, teachers, and explorers will be the next target to attract the displeasure of the powerful. The council is talking already of shutting down the royal archive and forcing the researchers to become librarians. The regents think this is a way to control us, to make us stick to the books they've approved instead of seeking out old stories or writing new ones. But the joke's on them. Now that I know our entire world was founded by a rebel librarian, I cannot think of a more noble job.

My apprenticeship is over. Now the real adventure begins.

I managed to smuggle a set of Waymaster's compasses out of the archive before the council could destroy them. I am including them in this box so that you, who have studied the Founders' secrets, may have the chance to try again—to stop the cycle of fear and secrecy and censorship. Maybe someday the people of Falinnheim will rediscover the stories of their past, so they can choose for themselves how to write their future.

Signed,

Iris the Irrepressible

Endeavor 2nd, 1114

———

No one said anything at first. Bastian stood behind Tuesday, reaching up to his shoulder to stroke Queen Elizardabeth thoughtfully with his index finger. Beside him, Zed rubbed Nyx's ears as she leaned against his leg. Tuesday sat on the planter ledge and read through the letter again, silently this time.

"Who is Iris the Irrepressible?" she asked, turning to Bastian. "Is she some explorer or historian you've studied with Gilford?"

"No idea," said Bastian. "I've never heard of her."

"Endeavor starts next week," Zed mused. "It might have been a day just like this when Iris wrote the book cipher and hid the box."

"How long ago was this?" Tuesday asked Bastian. "The date on the letter?"

Bastian squinted skeptically at her. "You don't know?"

"I'm still getting used to the new calendar," she retorted, her face reddening. "I get that Endeavor starts in the spring, but what year was it?"

"Falinnheim's years started counting from the date it was settled," he explained. "Well, *now* I know that. I guess growing up I never thought much about what that meant—the year was just a number. I should have realized the story didn't add up. Like, what happened *before* Year Zero? Did they want people to think Falinnheim just didn't exist, and then one day suddenly it did?"

Tuesday shot him a "get to the point" look.

"Anyway," Bastian finished, catching the hint, "1114 was just over a hundred years ago."

"So the war she mentioned, and the disease…"

"Probably the first World War," Zed finished for her. "And the flu epidemic of 1918."

"Wait, the *first* World War?" Bastian looked horrified. "Have there been more?"

Tuesday ignored the question. "1918…" she repeated. "Just like the old calendar you found."

Zed's eyebrows shot up. "The calendar right next to all those old Other Earth books."

Bastian stared at him. "Do you mean to say I've had Iris's collection sitting in the bunker this whole time?"

"Forget the books," said Tuesday. "Iris left us a set of compasses. We can go home!"

"Now hold on," said Zed. "Iris left the compasses so Falinnheim could be connected to the other Earth again. She wasn't sending whoever solved the book cipher on a private adventure—this is about *everyone*."

"Well 'everyone' isn't trapped in some weird alternate dimension where their whole life got turned upside down," Tuesday snapped. "I don't care what Iris had in mind. I've got a chance to get things back to normal, and I'm taking it."

Tuesday reached for the box she'd left on the planter ledge earlier.

The ledge was empty.

"Where did—?" Zed started. But he was interrupted by a rustling sound coming from a curtain of dangling vines to his right. The strands parted, and a man ducked out from between them.

A rather short, scruffy man wearing a stubbly beard and an apologetic grin.

"Awful sorry about this," said Scrimbley as he tucked the copper box into his cloak. "Truly, I am. But I has my orders."

"*Thief.*" Tuesday looked ready to spit venom. "We found that fair and square. Give it back!"

Bastian looked, bewildered, from Scrimbley to Nyx and back again. The hound wasn't growling, but she wasn't bounding up to greet Scrimbley, either. She just sat next to Zed, tongue lolling out, calmly watching Tuesday's temper boil over. "Why didn't Nyx notice you sneak in here?" he wondered aloud.

"Fairly certain she did," Scrimbley answered. "She just didn't let on about it."

"Why not?" asked Zed.

"I expect your mother told her not to. See, it's the hound's job to keep you safe from anything unexpected. And seeing as Her Highness is the one what ordered me to follow you around, that wasn't unexpected at all."

Tuesday's jaw dropped. "Mom did *what?*"

"Well, I guess technically the Princess didn't say *how* to solve her problem," Scrimbley clarified. "She hired me to search the palace for anything hidden in it what might be useful. Normally finding things everyone else overlooks is my specialty, but we're short on time, and I don't know my way around just yet. But you three seem to know every nook and corner of this place. So I figures, why not get you to do the searching for me? One sneak knows another, I always says. It was pretty clear you had your own puzzles brewing. Didn't take much of a nudge to get you working on mine."

Zed groaned. Back in the library, they thought they'd been outsmarting Scrimbley. Turns out they'd just taken his bait. Scrimbley didn't know which book gave the Princess her idea, or where the book was. And even if he had known, he couldn't get into the Princess's private study. But her children could.

Scrimbley had tricked them into doing his dirty work for him. And now the only working compasses in Falinnheim were sitting in his pocket.

CHAPTER 19
THE LAST STRAW

"I will never, ever forgive you."

Tuesday repeated the vow each time she caught sight of her mother. There was no point wasting her outrage on Scrimbley. Sneaking around spying on people and making shady deals for stolen goods was exactly the kind of behavior she expected from him. But she was determined to punish her mother's betrayal.

The Princess had no idea, of course, because Tuesday was no longer speaking to her. But that's what Tuesday would have said if she'd been feeling generous enough to say her threats out loud, instead of just rehearsing them in her mind.

No one bothered telling Tuesday, Zed, and Bastian about the latest developments in the ongoing palace drama, but as usual Bastian's access to the staff gossip train got them pretty well caught up. Scrimbley turned the compass set over to Princess Theadora, who smothered him with praise for finding a solution to her problem so quickly. Tuesday gave Iris's letter to Bastian for safekeeping, but apparently Scrimbley had learned enough from eavesdropping while she read it that he didn't need the actual papers—the moment he told Gilford there was a book of transporter coordinates somewhere in the royal archive, the librarian rushed out of the council meeting to track it down. Obaachan's mountain of supplies was loaded onto the hoversled Bastian's stepdad had modified to hide the contents, and an entire squadron of guards escorted it across town to Alexandria's jail. Then the guards returned with the (now empty) hoversled, the Princess's visitors dispersed, and the palace staff returned to their routines.

"It all fits," Bastian insisted as he shared the news with Tuesday and Zed the next morning. "Your mom had to figure out what to do with Tyrren after his trial, right? If he stayed in the capitol jail, sooner or later he'd bribe one of the jailers into letting him escape, or the Red Hand would sneak in and break him out. But when your mom read the story about everyone leaving Falinnheim to escape a volcano, she realized there was an unpopulated dimension she could send him to—she just had to figure out how to get there. So she hired Scrimbley to find her a working compass, and all the other experts prepared the stuff Tyrren would need to live 'Elsewhere', wherever that is."

"I guess that explains why Obaachan had the staff collecting so much food," Zed agreed. "Instead of keeping him in jail, they're stranding him someplace empty where he can't escape or cause any more trouble. I wonder why they needed a hologram programmer, though?"

"Didn't you say you once used a hologram to talk to people inside the Resistance base? Maybe they're doing the same thing—using a hologram to communicate with Tyrren from inside Falinnheim so they don't have to send real people over to guard him."

"When people have to spend too much time alone, they don't exactly… do well," Zed added. "Maybe they sent a hologram—or a bunch of holograms, even—to give Tyrren someone to talk to."

"One of the experts my mom had to track down was a psychologist," Bastian remembered. He laughed. "Maybe they programmed a hologram therapist who can talk Tyrren out of wanting to take over the world all the time."

"They're going to an awful lot of trouble to take care of a guy everybody hates," Tuesday grumped. "He doesn't deserve it."

"At least this way no one has to deal with him anymore," said Zed.

Gilford arrived to start the day's lessons, but no one bothered to hush up when he strolled through the library doorway. He already knew all their secrets.

They had expected the librarian to pretend everything was normal and forge ahead with the day's math, or science, or whatever lesson plan he had up his sleeve. But instead he slid into the seat across from Bastian and stared intensely at him from under furrowed gray eyebrows. "I'd like to ask you a favor," he said solemnly.

"Why bother asking?" Tuesday sulked. "Everybody seems pretty used to just taking things from us. And ordering us around. And barging in when we want privacy."

"I recognize that," said Gilford. "The developments this week have been important, but that doesn't give adults the right to walk all over you. Which is the reason I'm *asking*."

"Depends on the favor, I guess," Bastian answered.

"Scrimbley said there was a letter in the box you found in the conservatory. I'd like to read it. Please."

"Why?" said Tuesday. "So you can lock that away in the archives, too?"

Gilford must have been pretty desperate, because he completely ignored Tuesday's attitude. "I don't want to keep it," he said, nearly pleading now. "I just want to read it."

Bastian was silent for a moment, considering. Finally he reached into his book bag, took out *Grimm's Fairy Tales,* and flipped through the pages until he located Iris's letter sandwiched between them.

Gilford gently smoothed the creased papers out on the desktop. He read the letter in silence, his eyes combing eagerly through the lines of blue ink, drinking in every word. Then he handed the letter back to Bastian.

"Is that one of the books Iris brought back with her?" he asked as he watched Bastian slip the letter between Grimm's pages again.

"I think so. Zed and Tuesday say it comes from the other Earth, anyway."

"And you have more? From Nana Gertrude's trunk?"

Bastian nodded.

Tears welled in Gilford's eyes. "I wish I'd known sooner. I have so many questions for her. But it's too late now."

"I wish I could talk to her again too," said Bastian. "I'd love to know where she found all that stuff from her trunk."

"Not Nana Gertrude," said Gilford. "Iris. Your great-grandmother Gertrude was my mother. Her mother, Iris the Irrepressible, was my grandmother."

"Wait," Zed interrupted, "you actually *met* Iris?"

"I knew her well. Aside from seeing each other at family gatherings, Iris was the village librarian in my hometown for over sixty years. I went to the library every day after school." Gilford chuckled through his tears at the memory. "Every child in North Tarlington thought of Iris as their bonus grandmother. It made me something of a schoolyard celebrity to boast that she actually *was* mine."

"It's not fair," Tuesday broke in savagely. "None of it. Stealing people's family heirlooms, locking up all the books they didn't want people to read, lying about Falinnheim's entire history, forcing researchers to keep secrets from their own families… the Regents Council ruined Iris's life."

"Now, now," said Gilford. "I wish things had gone differently, but saying her life was *ruined* is a bit harsh. After all, Iris wrote that she was proud to be a librarian, even if she'd hoped to be an explorer instead. She's the reason *I* decided to become a librarian. She had passed on by the time I finished my apprenticeship, but if she was still with us, I think she'd be pleased to know her grandson went on to be the Royal Librarian. And in the end, I did get to hear her story."

"But no one else can!" Tuesday argued. "Iris is just as much a Founder as Olav, Edric, or Selene. Her adventure shaped Falinnheim's history. But no one knows about any of them because the government finds their stories inconvenient."

"I've been thinking about that, too," said Zed. "Take Obaachan, for example. She grew up in a village called Kyoto, where all her friends knew how to fold origami. And remember when she told us about her grandfather's slipsteel box? She said her great-uncle, the one who got the box open, was named Hiroshi. All of that sure sounds like stuff from Japan. But because the historians confiscated Kyoto's records, she doesn't know Japan exists! I mean, even her name—she said Obaachan means 'grandmother'. She thinks it's just a cute old-fashioned nickname. But it's actually Japanese, isn't it?"

Gilford nodded. "The village of Kyoto was settled by one of the Founders, Haruto the Valiant. I believe he named it in honor of the Other Earth city his entire refugee group came from. So it's likely that many people living in Kyoto today are the descendants of those settlers.

There are lots of little clues like that, all over Falinnheim. Village names, traditional stories and foods, local slang. I've always suspected they're remnants of a time when people understood their ancestors came from somewhere else. Perhaps a few words survived, preserved in popular culture like flies in amber, even though their context has been lost."

"Not lost," Tuesday argued. "*Stolen*. Iris was right—the regents may have thought they were protecting dangerous information, but by locking up people's stories, they stole the history and culture connected to those stories. And because of that, no one in Falinnheim understands who they really are. Those stories didn't belong to the regents— they belong to *everyone*. The regents had no right to take them away."

"I agree," said Gilford. "But we can't do anything to change that now."

"Do you think Nana Gertrude knew the books in her trunk were special?" Bastian asked. "Do you think Iris told her where they came from?"

"No idea. Mom certainly never told me about any of it, if she knew. I think it's more likely she kept the books for sentimental reasons—because she knew her mother loved them."

Bastian stared at his uncle. "Then why didn't *you* want them?"

"What?"

"After Nana Gertrude's funeral the whole family went through her things together. You and Grandpa Otto and Great Aunt Silvie got first choice of anything you wanted to keep. Why weren't the books important to you?"

"Well, I didn't know they were Other Earth artifacts," Gilford tried to explain.

"You're a librarian," Bastian countered. "*The* librarian. You love adding old books to your collection. You know that's not the reason. You just didn't think stories meant for children were important enough for the royal library."

Gilford held Bastian's stony stare. Uncle and nephew conducted a silent tug of war with their eyes, battling over which version of their shared history to declare the truth. But in only moments, Gilford relented. "You're right. If it had been Shakespeare, or Plato, or scientific or historical research, I would have wanted it. Perhaps I thought I'd outgrown the value of children's stories."

"Maybe if you'd actually read them, you would have figured out Iris's book cipher yourself. All the answers were there."

"I knew about the cipher," Gilford admitted. "I just didn't understand what it was. Thought some long-ago researcher had scribbled notes about other records to cross-reference or something. It never occurred to me that the numbers might be important. It seems my students could teach me a thing or two, in that regard."

Bastian sat thoughtfully for a moment, frowning slightly.

"You know what?" he said at last. "I think it's time I invited you to visit the bunker. I've got a little library of my own in there. I never got to meet Iris, but I got to know the stories she loved, and that's almost the same thing."

"I'd like that," said Gilford, wiping his eyes. "Thank you."

Everyone gathered their bookbags and followed Bastian and Nyx into the hall. "You know," Gilford added, "you've gotten quite the head start, for such a young book collector. Have you ever thought about becoming a librarian? I've been meaning to take on an apprentice."

"A librarian, huh?" Bastian grinned. "Sounds like an adventure."

———

Scrimbley and the rest of the Princess's visitors had been dismissed from the palace. Tyrren had been dismissed from Falinnheim. Bastian and Gilford were learning to work together. Baba still had a couple days left to hang out with Zed. All the palace guards and maids and mechanics returned to their regular duties. Coronation preparations were humming along. Yes, everything seemed to be shaping up splendidly.

For everyone but Tuesday.

First, the tailor's apprentice pulled Tuesday out of her afternoon chemistry lesson for another dress fitting. Nyx, who was (somehow) keeping an eye on Zed and Tuesday with her eyes closed (she was snoring under the library study table, as usual) followed Tuesday to the tailor's workshop.

As Tuesday had feared, the half-finished dress was the color of sea-monster snot and the ribbon trimming around the neckline was itchy. Even so, the dress's design wasn't turning out *that* bad—at least it had pockets. Definitely not the sort of thing she'd choose for herself, but as long as she was only required to wear the dress at the coronation ceremony, Tuesday decided she could live with that.

By the time Tuesday made it back to the library, the chemistry lesson was over. Zed informed her she'd missed a truly spectacular demonstration that sent a column of black foam spurting out of a beaker. Bastian informed her she'd missed Gilford's response to the unexpectedly dramatic chemical reaction, in which he'd made a noise like a mouse choking on a slide whistle.

Whatever. It couldn't have been as spectacular as the toothpaste volcano she and Orion had used on those invading soldiers back at the Resistance base. It was probably best Nyx hadn't been around for today's experiment anyway. Wouldn't want her getting spooked and bursting into flame, especially not in a library.

No, it wasn't slight annoyances like ugly dresses and missed excitement that finally got to Tuesday. The worst thing, the very last straw, was that her birthday was only two days away. And her mother already had the festivities planned out.

"It will be fabulous!" Mom insisted at the dinner table that evening. "Now that we're all settled back home, we can do a proper Falinnheim birthday celebration with all the traditional foods we couldn't get before: pickled gooseberries, smoked herring sandwiches, and a stewed chestnut tart with persimmon custard."

Tuesday was so shocked that she completely forgot she wasn't speaking to her mother. "What about cake and ice cream?" she asked. "Or pizza?"

"Don't be silly, dear. We don't do birthdays that way here."

"Falinnheim has something *like* pizza, I guess," her father added. "Flatbread with toppings, but there's usually no cheese."

"And of course we must have party games," Mom broke in. "Do you prefer Pass the Pudding or Three Ravens Shuffle?"

"I've never heard of either of those," said Zed.

"Never mind—we'll make time for both."

"Trying something new is all well and good," Obaachan counseled, "but birthdays are about tradition. A time to look behind you before tackling what lies ahead."

"Exactly!" said Tuesday. She knew Obaachan would talk some sense into Mom.

"I couldn't agree more," said the Princess. "Tradition. Precisely why this needs to be a classic Falinnheim celebration."

Obaachan raised an eyebrow and glanced between Tuesday and her mother but said nothing more.

"Sounds like *you'll* have a delightful time," Tuesday

grumbled to her plate. But no one heard her.

Tuesday moped through the rest of the meal. She moped up the stairs to her bedroom. She moped into her pajamas and moped dramatically onto her bed.

Hours passed. Tuesday stared at her ceiling, her mind pacing in circles as she recited her grievances. Somehow, she'd thought turning thirteen would change things—that her life would be different because *she'd* be different. But she saw the truth, now. Nothing was going to change. All she had to look forward to was another year of living in a house that would never feel like home, going to classes she didn't care about, to learn about a world she didn't belong in, to prepare for a job she didn't want.

No, not just another year. *All* the years. They'd planned out her entire life without so much as asking. It had started simply enough, but that was all part of the scheme. First it's an ugly dress and a bizarre birthday party, and before you know it you're stuck on the Regents Council with your mother as your boss, *forever*.

Iris was right. The people in charge never listened. Apparently not much had changed in the last hundred years.

Hundred? The past thousand, more like. Selene got roped into a life she didn't get to pick, either. Olav hadn't much cared where he ended up, so maybe he didn't mind the way his story turned out.

Maybe if Tuesday stopped caring where she ended up, she wouldn't mind either.

And Edric…

Edric!

Tuesday sat up in bed.

The people in charge had tried to plan out Edric's life for him, too. But unlike Iris or Olav or Selene, Edric hadn't gone along with it. Edric had chosen his own story.

Tuesday grabbed a crystal lantern from her bedside table, switched it on, and tiptoed out of her room.

CHAPTER 20
SLEEPWALKING

The hall was dark and quiet. Tuesday wrapped her hand around the glowing shard of crystal to block most of its light as she stalked silently past her parents' door. Nyx would be sleeping at the foot of their bed, as usual. If Tuesday was going to carry out her plan without Mom's furry spy tagging along, she would have to work through the night.

Out of the residence wing, down the cold stone steps, through the dim, empty corridors—Tuesday's bare feet seemed to have a mind of their own, carrying her along as though she'd paced this route a thousand times. When at last they stopped, she found herself in the portrait gallery, holding her lantern up to the very last painting.

Julian the Tinker. His story wasn't in *The Book of the Founders*, but somehow, Tuesday felt she knew him all the same. If Gilford was right, and Julian had ruled Falinnheim more than a thousand years ago, then he must be Olav and Selene's son. Or grandson, possibly. Either way, she was fairly certain he had known the Waymaster personally, which was probably where he got the idea to convert the rough lodestone-on-a-string into the first transporter compass. Gilford's history lesson had downplayed that in favor of the timekeeping invention—whether because the librarian didn't know about compasses at the time or because he didn't want to admit that he knew wasn't really important. The compass wouldn't appear in Julian's portrait if it wasn't significant.

She could only hope Gilford had been wrong about the next part.

In their first lesson, Gilford had insisted Julian's reign was too ancient for any of his artifacts to be preserved in the royal vault. But Scrimbley's compass was broken, and Iris's had been confiscated. The regents destroyed all the others a hundred years ago. Julian's, if it still existed, was her last hope.

Not that she had any idea where to find the vault, of course. Bastian might know that sort of thing, but now she was on her own.

What would Zed do? Tuesday closed her eyes and pictured herself asking her brother where the royal vault was likely to be.

In the palace somewhere, Imaginary Zed reasoned. It wouldn't make sense to put the vault someplace the regents would have to travel to access—that would draw too much attention. But where?

In the Moderator's quarters? If that was true, it torpedoed Tuesday's entire plan. She had no idea which rooms used to belong to the Moderator, back when there was one. She couldn't possibly search the residence wing right under everyone's snoring noses without getting caught.

Too obvious, said Imaginary Zed. Not secure enough. If the vault was on any of the upper floors, a thief could simply go to the floor below it and drill through the ceiling to break in. Tuesday was pretty sure she'd seen something like that in a heist movie.

The cellar, then.

Most of the palace's secret passages connected to the cellar because they were designed for the use of maids, cooks, and porters bustling back and forth from the cellar's workstations—the kitchens and linen closets and such. Tuesday decided to stick to the main hallways, though. She couldn't risk bumping into anyone who might be working late. Through the portrait gallery, down more flights of stairs, around the massive carved pillars in the entry hall, and through the swinging door to the service stairwell, Tuesday traced the path Bastian had shown her to the kitchens. She passed the laundry and the electrical control room, following the hall until she reached a door marked AUTHORIZED ACCESS ONLY.

This looked promising. Entry to the palace's secret passages and service stations was discouraged by hiding them in plain sight. None of it was off-limits to palace guests, exactly, just designed so their eyes would slide right over it. Whatever waited behind this door was actually forbidden. So whatever was inside, it had to be important.

The door was locked, of course. Tuesday tried her key to the residence wing, hoping it was some sort of master design that fit every lock in the palace. It wouldn't even slide into the keyhole.

Tuesday couldn't say why the thought came to her. Perhaps the situation was just close enough to the last time she'd been trying to break into a locked room to jog her memory. If the library's historical archive was protected by a slipsteel lock, couldn't the royal vault be, too? If Bastian's resonance was close enough to the Royal Librarian's to fool the slipsteel, then maybe hers was similar enough to the Captain of the Guard. Or the Regent. It didn't matter which of her parents the lock was calibrated for, actually— her resonance should be a perfect mix of the two.

She laid her hand on the doorknob and imagined the lock's tumblers turning to draw in the deadbolt. There was a faint clicking noise, and when she tried the knob again, it turned.

Behind the door, Tuesday found yet another dark hallway. She raised the crystal lantern for a better look, but its pink glow illuminated only the next few steps in front of her. After following the straight, bare corridor for barely a minute, she looked back over her shoulder and realized she could no longer see the door behind her. She wasn't likely to lose her way in the dark, since there were no doorways to choose from or corners to turn, but her stomach dropped all the same. Nothing to do but keep walking, now. If she lost her nerve and kept looking back, she might get turned around and lose track of which direction went ahead, and which was her path back to the rest of the palace.

After what seemed an eternity with only her echoing footsteps for company, Tuesday finally reached a new landmark. The passage became a set of stone steps descending even further below the cellar level, and at the bottom of the steps she found another locked door. Unlike the plain metal door she'd encountered last time, this one was bordered with ornate geometric ironwork. And stamped into the very center: a pair of ravens, their bodies overlapping but their beaks facing away from each other, as though looking over each other's shoulders to check that they weren't being watched.

The royal crest! This *had* to be the vault.

Tuesday wiped her sweating palm on her pajamas and laid her hand on the doorknob.

At that exact moment, someone laid a hand on her shoulder.

Tuesday screamed and dropped her lantern. She whirled around, but with the lantern on the floor all she could see was a huge pair of black leather boots.

The boots' owner stooped to pick up the lantern. A gloved hand slowly raised the glowing crystal over Tuesday's head, revealing a tall, cloaked body, and then a face: a broad nose, warm brown skin, and a pair of dark eyes that somehow managed to radiate annoyance, concern, and amusement at the same time.

Tuesday knew that face. "Captain Solomon!"

Trapped between the horror of being startled in the dark, the embarrassment of getting caught snooping, and the relief of finding some friendly company in the spooky passageway, Tuesday's instinctive reaction surprised both of them: she wrapped her arms around the guard's middle and hugged him. She wasn't happy, exactly. In fact, if the sinking sensation in her stomach was any indication, she was about to be in a lot of trouble. But if she *had* to be discovered breaking into an obviously-off-limits area of the palace in the dead of night, she was glad her friend from the Resistance base was the one to do it.

"It's Lieutenant Solomon now," the man chuckled. "I don't work for the General anymore, remember? Your father's the Captain."

Tuesday hadn't realized Solomon worked in the palace at all. But of course, since the Resistance had disbanded after Tyrren's arrest, it made sense their top agent would be looking for a new position. The Royal Guard was a perfect fit for his skills. Not to mention her father, tasked with rooting out corruption in the ranks, had been in desperate need of trusted guards. He'd probably recruited Solomon personally.

"What are you doing here?" Tuesday asked when she finally released Solomon.

"My job, obviously. The Royal Guard has me on night patrol. Though, funny enough, I was about to ask you the same thing."

Tuesday glanced down at her pajama-clad legs and bare feet. "Would you believe… sleepwalking?"

Solomon smiled and shook his head.

"You're not going to tell my mom, are you?"

"Your mother? Certainly not. *You're* going to do that. Right after I report to my commanding officer."

Tuesday's stomach plunged even deeper. He meant Dad.

"I promise there's a good explanation," Tuesday assured him.

Solomon laughed. "Can't wait to hear it. Now come on— let's have this conversation somewhere a little less creepy."

Tuesday waited in the kitchen while Solomon made his report. Rather than trekking all the way to the seventh floor, he pulled a portable hologram projector out of a supply cabinet and switched it on. Tuesday was expecting a glowing green character to appear and start reciting programmed phrases, but instead Solomon stepped into the beam of light and stated his request that Captain Beren come to the kitchen to be briefed on "a security discovery of a sensitive nature."

"Your father had a matching projector installed in his

quarters," Solomon explained when he switched the unit off again and joined Tuesday at the kitchen counter. "If I've done this right, he should be seeing and hearing me as though we're in the same room."

"I've never seen a hologram used like that before," said Tuesday. "In fact, I don't think I've noticed *any* holograms in the palace."

"This was just installed a couple days ago, actually. I hear a Hololab technician came up with the idea while he was here consulting on a different matter, so he asked the Royal Guard to test out the prototype. Usually holograms have to be programmed in advance, but he realized the same equipment could be used to deliver live messages from one projector to another. Saves a lot of time walking through all the corridors to find the person you want to talk to."

Solomon went to loot through the refrigerator and returned with a wedge of cheese, a jar of pickled plums, and a spiced pear cake with several slices already missing. Tuesday stared in disbelief as he assembled a plate with a little bit of everything and plopped down on the tall counter stool next to hers. "How can you eat at a time like this?"

"Figured this was as good a time as any for my lunch break. But my lunch can be your midnight snack—join me! Besides, if you're going to have an unpleasant conversation, there's no sense making it more unpleasant by being hungry. It's remarkable how a simple snack can grease the wheels of conversation."

"Easy for you to say," Tuesday grumbled. "Dad will probably end up awarding you a medal or something. I'm going to be grounded for the rest of my life."

"Don't be silly. Your father can't ground you for the rest of your life. Only for the rest of *his* life."

"Thanks, that's loads better. Only fifty years or sixty years to go, then."

By the time Captain Beren arrived, his uniform jacket and boots hastily thrown on over his pajamas, Solomon and Tuesday were on their second slices of cake. Solomon stood, saluted, then cut yet another slice and slid the plate across the counter. Beren ate in silence while his lieutenant explained how he'd noticed light under the door of the restricted access hall and followed it, matching the intruder's footsteps so he wouldn't be heard, and discovered Tuesday attempting to enter the royal vault.

"I imagine she would have succeeded, given enough time," Solomon concluded. "She'd already made it past the access door."

"We've really got to track down the steelsmith Tyrren was using," Beren sighed. "I can't believe we're still working off locks that were tuned twenty years ago. That's a major security flaw."

"Wait," said Tuesday. "You mean the slipsteel in the access door and the vault isn't tuned to you and Mom? How did I get the door open, then?"

"The slipsteel in the access door was tuned to the previous Captain of the Royal Guard—my father. And the vault was tuned to the last Moderator—Mom's grandfather. There was no connection between our families at the time. You just happen to be descended from both men, so apparently both locks work for you."

"We know Tyrren had access to a steelsmith," Solomon added, "because new members of the Legion were getting slipsteel swords made. But we don't know who it was. We can't make swords for the new guards or update the locks until we find the missing steelsmith."

"Why didn't Tyrren have the locks changed?" Tuesday asked.

"No idea," said Beren. "The vault doesn't have money in it, though. The royal accounts are at the Alexandria bank. Maybe family heirlooms weren't the kind of treasure Tyrren cared about."

Tuesday tried to come up with more questions to delay the proceedings, but too late—Dad pulled out the hologram unit and called for Mom to join them in the kitchen. And apparently she wanted backup, because when Princess Theadora arrived, Nyx and Baba were right behind her.

Solomon passed around more cake. When at last everyone was seated around the kitchen counter, all eyes turned to Tuesday.

There was no more putting it off. Tuesday gulped, set down her fork, and tried to find the words. Explaining where she'd been going was straightforward enough. It was a lot tougher to make them understand *why*. Partly because Tuesday wasn't entirely sure of that, herself.

But of course, a pause to collect her thoughts only created an opening for Mom to cut in. "There isn't a compass in the vault anyway," she informed Tuesday. "You really think I hadn't considered that already? When Gilford and Scrimbley told me neither of them had a compass, that was the first place I checked."

"Can't you just give me two seconds to talk?" Tuesday erupted. "Ever since you got put in charge you think you can order everybody around! I'm done putting up with it. I'm not going to be quiet and polite and obedient. I'm done with dog nannies and ugly dresses and weird birthdays. And I'm not joining your dumb Regents Council, *ever*."

"Whoa!" Dad interrupted. "You can't talk to your mother like that."

"Maybe it's about time someone did! No one dares to say what they really think because they're not allowed to argue with a princess. Well, I'm not afraid to tell you things you don't want to hear. You think manners and traditions are all that matter, but they're not. You have no idea what it's like having your whole life planned out for you."

Without a word, Princess Theadora stood and left the kitchen, Nyx padding along behind her. She didn't cry. She didn't scold or argue or make excuses. She just left.

"You make some valid points," said Baba mildly,

taking another bite of cake. "Life in the palace has been a big change, and people have new expectations of you. The adults in your life have been doing an awful lot of telling, and not much asking or listening. Still, it's rather ironic. None of us know what it's like to grow up in this massive old house and be expected to follow in your family's footsteps. But your mother does. She was a young princess once too, you know. You've just lectured the only person in Falinnheim who actually *does* understand what you're going through."

CHAPTER 21
ONE LAST SECRET

Baba finished her cake, bid Beren and Solomon good night, and calmly escorted Tuesday back to the residence wing.

Tuesday paused outside the door to her parents' quarters. "Do I have to?"

"No, actually," said Baba. "I won't make you do anything. But I guarantee this conversation will go better tonight than it will if you put it off. Ignoring problems doesn't make them go away. It just gives them time to fester."

"Will you at least come with me?"

"Sorry. You and your mother need to solve this one yourselves." Baba patted her on the shoulder and returned to the guest room.

When Tuesday was alone again, she finally worked up the nerve to knock. But before her knuckles could make contact with the door, her mother called, "Come in."

Tuesday found her mother seated at a writing desk in the lounge. "How did—?" she started to ask.

"Nyx," Mom answered simply. She gestured to the hound, who had already made herself comfortable on the sofa.

"I didn't think you'd invite me in. Seeing as you walked off last time I tried talking to you."

"I needed to calm down before I said something I'd regret. Princesses aren't allowed to lose their cool. Or at least, I wasn't ever allowed to."

"Look, I'm sorry I yelled," said Tuesday. "But I still mean what I said. I know you spent years missing Falinnheim and you're happy to be back, but it's not *my* home. Everything might be going great for *you*, but—"

"Everything's not going great," said Mom. "I thought moving back home and defeating Tyrren would solve all my problems, but it turns out there are always new ones."

"Like what?" asked Tuesday skeptically.

Princess Theadora pointed to a stack of papers on the desk. "This job isn't meant to be done by just one person. Growing up, I expected to get decades of experience helping my parents, siblings, and cousins on the Regents Council, but they're all gone. I thought assembling a team of advisors would help, but they all have their own ideas about how to run things. I've got petitions from village councils all over Falinnheim trying to tell me what to do.

"Some activist in Persepolis claims our whole family should be quarantined or we'll spread diseases from the other Earth—never mind that we've been in Falinnheim half a year already. The mayor of New Athens insists that because you and Zed weren't born in Falinnheim you're not actually citizens and shouldn't be allowed to join the Regents Council when you grow up. The village council in Etrusia wants the exact opposite—they argue that because I'm the only royal left, it's my duty to have a bunch more children to build the future Regents Council."

"Wow, that's… really messed up." Tuesday thought being told what to wear was bad enough. She couldn't imagine being surrounded by people who wanted to control major life decisions like that.

"Maybe you don't have to do *any* of it," Tuesday suggested. "I mean, maybe Falinnheim would be better off not having royalty at all. You could set up some other system, then we could go back home and it wouldn't be your problem anymore."

"Believe me, I considered that. I spent the entire time we lived in the other Earth studying various countries' methods of government, but they all have their flaws. Any time people are born into power, they're tempted to use it to get more power. But in places that choose presidents and prime ministers and such, only the most ambitious run for election in the first place, so the result is often the same—people are in charge because they love being in charge, not because they're any good at it. I'm not saying Falinnheim's way of running things is perfect—no system of government is—but at least with a council and a moderator, we're trying to prevent any one person from getting too much control. And there's something to be said for spending your entire adolescence preparing to serve your people, rather than just being rich or charismatic enough to convince people to vote for you."

"I guess. Whatever. I'm not trying to change the world, Mom. I just want to go home."

"Is that why you were trying to find a transporter compass? Because you're homesick?"

Tuesday sighed. "I guess so. The idea of digging up a compass and going back all by myself might sound stupid, but I just felt like no one ever listened to me, and if I didn't get to choose something for myself, I'd explode."

"I think if you'd succeeded, you'd have run into a bunch of problems pretty quickly—how to get food, and money, and stay safe. It was a reckless thing to do. But I definitely understand how you're feeling. And you're right, I got so caught up in my own problems that I wasn't paying attention to how that affected you. I'm sorry I haven't been listening."

"It's pretty hard to listen when we never actually talk," Tuesday sulked. "Our family has a long history of keeping secrets. Zed and I have been doing it too, I guess. But none of it worked out like we hoped. I mean, if we'd all been working together, we could have read *The Book of the Founders* and solved Iris's riddle and found a way to manage Tyrren without wasting all this time spying on each other. Refusing to talk about uncomfortable things didn't solve our problems—it created new ones."

Her mother sat in silence for a long while. Tuesday fought the temptation to argue her point further; she let her words hang in the tense silence, filling every corner of the room like a thick fog.

"You're right," her mother said. "Perhaps it's time we learned about each other by actually sharing, instead of sneaking around trying to discover each other's mysteries. Tell our stories freely, instead of trying to solve one another like puzzles."

The Princess dug into the desk drawer and pulled out a stack of handwritten pages. She moved to the sofa, gently nudging Nyx aside to make room to sit. Then she rifled through the papers, frowning in thought as she removed some and kept others, before handing her selections to her daughter.

"My advisors suggested Dad and I add our stories to *The Book of the Founders*. How we left Falinnheim, and came back, and defeated Tyrren. I can't let you read all of it yet," she explained, heading off Tuesday's objection. "For one thing, we haven't finished writing it. And some parts of the story are still classified. Maybe later I can make you a copy with individual words blacked out, but for now let's just stick to the pages that are definitely kid-friendly. The missing sections will create a few gaps in the story, but it's better than nothing."

"There can't be *that* many secrets," Tuesday said, eyeing the pages her mother had kept back. "At least not secrets that are new to me. I mean, technically everything about the other Earth is still classified, but it's a little late to keep me from knowing about that, seeing as I spent my whole life there."

The Princess frowned. "It's not that. There are a couple of details we need to stop from spreading until we can locate the rest of the Red Hand, but mostly… well, it's the same reason I refused to involve you in Tyrren's trial. This is the whole truth in here, every detail of the attack, and I can't burden you with that knowledge."

"I can handle it!" Tuesday protested. But her mother shook her head.

"You are young. Your emotions are raw and tender and reactive, which is exactly what makes you different from the people who carried out these attacks. Tyrren's followers only agreed to his plan because a lifetime of selfish ambition made them numb to cruelty. Your sensitivity is a *gift*. It would be a terrible shame to dull it by exposing it to such violence, even in a book. But even with the traumatic parts removed, there is enough of the story left to help you understand."

Tuesday nodded and accepted the pages. She briefly considered taking them back to her bedroom, or the library, or even the bunker, to read them in private. But the same instant the thought arrived, she sent it on its way. No—they'd had enough secrecy, enough solitude. It was time to do something together.

Tuesday plopped down on the sofa next to her mother and began to read.

CHAPTER 22
THE TALE OF THE
MISSING REGENT

It was going to be a great day. Beren could feel it.

It had taken five years of apprenticeship to get promoted to a full member of the Royal Guard. Two more years went by before he got his first solo assignment. Another two were spent rotating between various palace stations. But today, finally, it was his turn. He was being trusted to protect the Moderator. And not at some regular council meeting, either. Today was a royal accession ceremony. Today was special.

Beren woke up early so he could take his time getting ready, polishing his boots and the brass buttons on his uniform with extra care. He was just buckling his slipsteel sword into place when Captain Argo strode into the deserted barracks common room.

"Beren," said the Captain as they exchanged salutes. "I have a special assignment for you."

"Of course. Anything you need, sir."

The Captain nodded. "I knew I could count on you."

But the triumphant smile drained from Beren's face as Captain Argo finished his request. "We will be switching duty assignments today."

It was a command, not a question, and Beren knew it. Arguing with the Captain wasn't going to get him anything but a tour of duty scrubbing the barracks latrine. Still, he couldn't hide his disappointment. He phrased his response carefully, making his objection known without actually refusing the new orders. "I can serve admirably in any assignment," he said with another salute, "including protecting the Moderator."

Captain Argo smiled and patted him on the shoulder. "I know you can. Which is why I've decided to give you my own duty station, guarding the new regent."

"As you wish, Captain. Shall I inform Lieutenant Sylas of the change?"

For the first time, the Captain's armored confidence dulled. "No," he said after a pause. "I'll make all the arrangements—no need to bother Sylas with it. You'll get another assignment with the Moderator soon, I'm sure. But today, I need to guard him myself."

Again, Beren risked a question. "Is something wrong?"

The Captain shook his head. "Just got a funny feeling

about today, that's all." He laughed and clapped Beren on the shoulder again. "Spare an old soldier one day to indulge his intuition. When it comes to nothing, as I'm sure it will, you can have your pick of assignments."

"Yes, Captain."

Captain Argo turned to leave, then paused as though he had forgotten something. He doubled back and wrapped Beren in a hug. "I'm so proud of you, son. You know that, don't you?"

The abrupt abandoning of protocol caught Beren off guard—which was ironic, as his skill in staying *on guard* was the thing he valued most in the world. He and Captain Argo had agreed years ago on keeping strict professional boundaries to avoid the appearance of favoritism. But they were alone. Just this once, Beren decided, it couldn't hurt to let his guard down.

Beren returned the hug. "Thank you, Dad. I'm proud of you, too."

Those were the last words they ever spoke to each other.

———

Knock. Knock, knock-knock.

"Coming, Eunice!" Princess Theadora rushed to unbolt her bedroom door. "I know it's a special occasion, but don't you think six o'clock is a bit early? Whatever fancy new hairstyle you've got in mind can't possibly take *that* lo—" She flung the door open but flinched backward when she came face to face not with Eunice, but with a dark-haired young soldier. She didn't know his name, since he hadn't been assigned as her bodyguard before, but Theadora was certain she'd seen him standing at attention in various corners of the palace grounds. "You're not my hairdresser," was all she could think to say.

The soldier frowned. "No, Your Highness."

Theadora suddenly became aware she was still in her dressing gown and slippers. Which was a totally normal thing to be wearing when breakfast was an hour away, let alone any official duties, but still—awkward. Nothing to be done about that now, though. There was only one option left to salvage her dignity: pretend she didn't care. She smiled warmly at her unexpected visitor as though she always took social calls in her pajamas. "Can I help you with something?"

"No, Your Highness. I'm your security escort for the day. Just wanted to let you know I had arrived for duty a bit early."

"I thought the Captain was supposed to look after me today," said Theadora.

"Yes, Your Highness. I mean—no, Your Highness."

"Well, which is it?"

"The Captain was assigned to escort you to the Regents Council ceremony, but there's been a change of plans. Don't worry, you won't notice any difference to your schedule today. Just pretend I'm not here."

"That's going to be pretty difficult, considering we're

in the middle of a conversation. I don't make a habit of talking to myself." This was a lie—Theadora was fairly sure *everyone* talked to themselves, at least sometimes—but she was also fairly certain most people didn't like to admit it. Besides, it was a princess's job to act like everything was under control, and this interaction was getting off on the wrong foot.

The soldier suppressed a sigh. "Yes, Your Highness. I'll be stationed just outside the door, here. Please inform me when you're ready to leave."

Theadora laughed. "I'd have a pretty hard time leaving without you, seeing as you're guarding the only way out."

That was a lie, too. But the soldier wouldn't know that, and she wanted to close the door on the awkward encounter. She wasn't going to let a little hiccup like this set her day on the wrong track. After all, it's not every day you get named a regent. And it was her birthday, besides.

Theadora carried on with her morning routine, scrubbing her face and slipping on the new emerald-green dress the royal tailor had made her for the occasion. She applied a generous layer of her favorite orange-scented hand lotion before wiggling the ring bearing her family crest onto her index finger.

She was just starting to brush out her hair when a muffled voice floated in from the hallway. Perfect timing! This time, it was sure to be Eunice.

It wasn't.

Theadora unbolted the door again. For a moment, all she could do was stand in the doorway and stare while her brain tried to make sense of the scene that greeted her.

Her guard had his sword drawn, locked in a stalemate against an identical blade held by an older, taller soldier. She recognized this one—he was the Royal Guard's second-in-command and had been on her security detail many times before.

"Lieutenant Sylas… what's going on?"

Both men looked up at her in surprise.

"Your Highness," said the lieutenant in his smooth, emotionless voice, "the palace is under attack. Your guard may be one of the conspirators. I need you to move away from him, or he will try to use you as a shield. Don't panic. I'll hold him back—just step into the hall and get behind me."

"Don't listen to him," the younger guard pleaded through gritted teeth. "*He's* the attacker! Stay in your room and bolt the door."

The two men had their swords crossed in front of their chests, standing so close they could have whispered to each other. Each was straining to shove the other back with his sword to open up enough room for a proper attack, but they were deadlocked.

"Princess," Sylas ordered, "I'm trying to protect you. Come here. Now."

Theadora's eyes darted from the determined expression on Sylas's face to the younger guard's barely restrained panic.

Then she noticed a clean slice through the shoulder of the young guard's uniform, the edges slowly seeping red.

Clanging sounds and distant shouts drifted in from the corridors beyond.

"Close the door!" her guard yelled.

"You have to make a decision," said Sylas patiently, still resisting his opponent's blade. "Who are you going to trust?"

The young guard had shown up early, unannounced, to alter the day's security plan. Last-minute changes were definitely suspicious. And she'd known Sylas since she was a child…

But then she caught the red streaks on Sylas's sword and the eager gleam in his eye, like he was hypnotically willing her to step into the hall.

Sylas was never eager.

She made her choice.

Without a word, Theadora threw her hairbrush at Sylas, catching him square in the face. As Sylas stumbled, she grabbed the other guard by the collar of his uniform and yanked him two steps back, through the doorway.

"That was foolish," the man said as Theadora bolted the door. "It's my job to protect *you*—don't put yourself at risk trying to help. And besides, you *don't* actually know which of us to trust."

Theadora felt strangely calm. Logically, she understood that she and the guard were both in incredible danger, but perhaps the reality of the situation hadn't yet settled in.

"Well, seeing as you haven't attacked me yet," she told him, "I think it's fair to say my gamble paid off. If I'd left you in the hallway to battle it out, Sylas might have won. Then I'd be trapped in here while he tries to break the door down."

There was a massive thud against the solid oak slab that made the hinges rattle. "Pretty sure he's going to do that anyway," said the soldier.

"Yes," Theadora argued, "but now someone on *this* side of the door is armed."

They worked together to shove the massive trunk at the foot of her bed in front of the door. Then the soldier peered through the black-paned window on the opposite wall, out to the courtyard below.

"No point waiting here to be attacked again," he said. "It's only one floor down to that balcony. Too far to jump, but maybe if we tie blankets or something into a rope…"

"Or we could just walk." Theadora crossed the room and pointed to the tall, gold-framed mirror next to her closet. The frame was secured to the wall, but when she pressed on the glass it swung inward on hidden hinges, revealing a staircase.

The soldier transformed his slipsteel sword into a hammer, which he used to shatter the window. Then he snatched a blanket off the bed, tied one end to the bedpost, and dangled the rest out the opening to the balcony below.

"What are you doing?" Theadora hissed. "Come on!"

"Sylas is going to get in here eventually—better to let

him *think* he knows where we went than to wonder how we got out and start investigating. Sending him down to the balcony will buy us some time."

They ducked into the mirror frame, closing the glass behind them, and started down the stairs.

"Thank you, by the way," Theadora whispered. "For saving my life and all."

"Maybe wait to thank me until we're actually out of the palace. A lot could go wrong before then, Your Highness."

"Quit calling me that!" she protested. "Theadora's fine."

"As you like. When we get to the end of this tunnel, a lot could still go wrong, *Theadora*."

"Fine. If it all goes horribly wrong, who should I blame? I don't even know your name."

The soldier managed a grim smile. "Beren, Your Highness. Call me Beren."

———

"'Got to leave Alexandria,' you said. 'Better sell your fancy dress and find something boring to wear so we'll blend in,' you said. Fat lot of good that did us!"

"It was a good plan!" Beren argued. "How could I have known the only other customer in the thrift shop was a bandit?"

A rich, rolling laugh echoed through the cave. "A bandit?" their captor repeated. "You'll have to excuse my vanity, but I think Osiris the Merciless qualifies for a more interesting title than a simple bandit. I'd much prefer 'scourge of the south' or 'notorious criminal mastermind.' Something with a bit of flair."

Beren was still smarting about getting captured, but he couldn't help being impressed. "Wait—*you're* Osiris the Merciless?"

The bald, mustachioed man before them took a theatrical bow.

Theadora twisted in her ropes to get a better look at the famous outlaw. "I thought Osiris the Merciless was supposed to lead some sort of fearsome gang," she said. "But you're the only person here."

Osiris chuckled. "The only *person,* yes. But I assure you, the gang is plenty fearsome."

He didn't call, or whistle, or make any command at all. And yet right on cue, six enormous black beasts stalked silently in from a side chamber, their eyes glowing ominously blue through the shadows. Theadora would have called them wolves, and yet—no. She may only have heard of wolves in stories, but all the same, she was certain these creatures were nothing like them. These could only be Gabriel Hounds.

"So what is it?" Osiris continued. "What's got you ducking through backwater villages and pawning your fancy clothes? Are you running off to elope, or something?"

They were tied up back-to-back, but that didn't stop Theadora and Beren from craning toward each other to exchange looks of pure disdain.

"Are you joking?" Theadora asked. "We only met today."

"I'd rather drink my own bath water," Beren declared.

Osiris reached over to stroke the fur of the nearest hound. "Well whatever you've done to upset the snooty capitol crowd, it appears they want you returned to them. A bunch of wanted posters matching your descriptions just went up in the village square. You're only worth fifty Hours each, at the moment. It's curious, though—the posters don't include your names, or even what you're wanted *for*. I'm guessing that's because they don't want to admit how valuable you really are. I can negotiate a deal worth ten times that. So if you'll excuse me, it appears I need to send a letter to Alexandria."

Osiris strolled away, still laughing, but two of the hounds stayed behind to supervise the captives.

"So," Theadora whispered. "Got any other 'good' ideas?"

"That depends," said Beren. He tucked one leg behind him so the guard hounds couldn't see it. "Can you reach my boot? I've got a rock stuck down the top of the left one and it's driving me nuts. See if you can get it out."

"What good will that do?"

"Well for one, I'll be a lot more comfortable."

Theadora rolled her eyes, but strained against the ropes until her fingers found the offending stone. She dropped it in the dust beside them.

Beren picked it back up.

"Your arms are tied down," she reminded him (as

though he could have forgotten.) "You won't be able to throw it at the hounds."

"Throw it?" Beren whispered. "Now why would I want to do that?"

Silently, he transformed the heavy gray stone back into a formless blob of slipsteel, which hardened into a jagged-toothed knife. Beren twiddled his fingers, awkwardly maneuvering the small blade into place. Slowly, ever so slowly, he began sawing through the ropes.

––––––

"What's taking so long?" Beren hissed. "Any second now, the whole thing's going to explode!"

Theadora gazed across the wall of flames. They'd started out eerily blue, but the fire sparked by Osiris's hounds had spread to the cave's living quarters. Everything was blazing orange, now. Beren was right— the next chamber was the armory. Once the fire reached that barrel of cannon powder…

She turned to make her escape, but the pile of blankets was still whimpering.

No, she told herself. It was a monster. Even if it was a cute, helpless, baby monster. Sure, it didn't seem threatening now, but someday it would grow up to be exactly like its parents. She could not save it.

The sleek black puppy poked its head out of the blanket. It whimpered again.

Beren was still waiting at the mouth of the cave. "Let's

go!" he called.

Theadora scooped up the tiny Gabriel Hound and hid it under her cloak.

————

"It's not going to work," said Beren.

"Sure it will," Theadora insisted. "We just have to hurry. Scrimbley said the Placid Perfume lasts about two hours. We've already used twenty minutes of that getting here."

Theadora wished she felt as confident as she sounded. The smuggler had been right about the compass though—and if Scrimbley could pull off something as impossible as traveling between worlds, then his plan to get them new identities should be a piece of cake. All they had to do was go to the office and sign a few papers. Everyone standing nearby would smell the perfume, which would make them irresistibly agreeable. They'd approve the documents without any fuss at all.

"Too bad getting doused in that stuff didn't make *you* any more agreeable," Beren muttered. "Then I could talk you into ditching that… *beast*."

Theadora squinched up her eyes at him, then stroked the furry black lump snoring in her satchel. "Good thing Scrimbley already gave us the antidote. Besides, it's my birthday. You wouldn't make me give up my birthday present, would you?"

"Your birthday was yesterday," he argued. "And no one *gave* that monster to you—you stole it."

"*Rescued* it," she corrected. "And I'm pretty sure it was before midnight, so it was still my birthday at the time."

There was no point arguing. Beren knew she could play the "princess card" if she wanted and order him to drop his objection. But she hadn't. Theadora might be annoying, and naive, and dangerously optimistic, but at least she never pulled rank on him.

Just as Scrimbley had predicted, everyone at the registration office was welcoming to the point of being ridiculous. No one noticed the strangers' odd clothing, or questioned why they had no idea where to go or what to do. From the customers waiting in line to the employees stationed behind the long gray counter, everyone wore dreamy grins and glassy eyes as Beren and Theadora strolled in and made their requests. Yes, of course! They'd be delighted to make new government ID cards! No birth certificates, proof of address, or proof of existence? No problem! No money? Good thing everything is free today, for some reason! Wait, is that a puppy in your bag? Yes, of course dogs are allowed inside. In fact, go ahead and skip to the front of the line—we *all* want a look at the puppy!

Unfortunately, though the smuggler's perfume worked wonders on government employees, it couldn't do anything about government paperwork. As Theadora retreated to a corner desk to fill out her forms, she realized she had a problem.

"*Last* name?" she whispered to Beren, pointing as she

read off the paper. "How many names do these people use, anyway? And I don't see any place to list a title."

"I think the last one is a family name," he said. "But apparently the names need to be in the right order? The lady at the desk told us to fill in the forms 'last name first', whatever that means."

"Last name first…" Theadora repeated. After a moment of thought, a grin spread across her face. She plopped down in the seat next to Beren and wrote out her new name.

LAST NAME: FURST

FIRST NAME: ZORA

"That's… actually really clever," Beren was forced to admit.

"You'll have to come up with your own idea for a last name," Theadora told him. "Unless you want to pretend our secret identities are siblings or something. Or married, I guess."

"Not in a million years," said Beren. "It's bad enough we're stuck together in a weird secret land—no need to make this any more miserable. I wouldn't even *pretend* to be married to you."

Theadora laughed. "Agreed. You may be cute, but you're not *that* cute."

"Let's just hope we're not stuck here very long, then."

The fugitives sealed their pact with a handshake and returned to their paperwork.

CHAPTER 23
A BIRTHDAY SURPRISE

And that was the end of the story. Or at least the end of what was written so far.

"Ugh, *Mom*!" Tuesday protested when she finished gagging. "I thought this was supposed to be a daring escape adventure story. Did you really have to make it so… mushy?"

"Excuse me," her mother laughed, "but this is not just *any* mushy story. This is the story of how your parents met. If we'd never met you wouldn't be here at all, so be grateful. Besides, it's not like there's kissing or anything."

"You didn't have to put in all the flirty fake arguing, though. You could have summarized. And besides, just because it happened doesn't mean you have to put it in a history book! Olav and Selene got married eventually, and their story was way less embarrassing."

"Olav and Selene's story wasn't adapted for the book

until hundreds of years later. I got to write my own story, so I can put in all the cute banter I want."

Actually, Tuesday decided, she wouldn't have minded *so* much if Olav and Selene's story had included a bit more romance. It was reading about her *parents'* budding romance that made her cringe.

Tuesday had expected the boys to agree with her, but when she filled them in the next morning, they didn't seem to get it.

"So what?" was all Zed had to say.

"That's totally normal," Bastian insisted. "I don't know how it works out in real life, but in books, the best indication a couple is going to end up together is that they spend the first half of the story arguing."

"Read a lot of romance novels, do ya?" Tuesday teased.

Bastian just shrugged. "Shakespeare," he explained. "If the story is a tragedy, it's love at first sight. If it's a comedy, they can't stand each other."

"You're right," said Tuesday. "A story where a bunch of people get killed and a dictator takes over definitely sounds like a comedy."

———

Tuesday waited for her punishment to be handed down, but it never came. Her father informed her over lunch that Solomon, Baba, and Obaachan had negotiated a deal in her favor. Since she already spent all her time in the palace, they argued, in a way she had been grounded for weeks without even knowing it. Clearly, restricting her privileges wasn't helpful. Perhaps it was time to try something different.

"Different how?" Tuesday asked warily.

Zed looked mystified too, but everyone else at the table exchanged conspiratorial grins. Then Obaachan reached under her chair and pulled out a purple box tied with a silky ribbon bow. "We decided you might like to open your birthday present a day early," she said with a wink.

Tuesday untied the ribbon and lifted the lid from the box. Inside she found two round, shiny gold spheres nestled into a bed of crinkled-up crepe paper.

"Are these—?"

Princess Theadora nodded. "Iris's compasses. I truly didn't ask Scrimbley to spy on you to get them—I thought he'd be searching the palace for hidden compartments. Finding the compasses was important, but I'm sorry it happened in a way that left you feeling disrespected."

"Now this is a loan, you understand," Beren added, "not a gift. But we figured since you kids were the ones to discover them, it's only fair you should get to take them for a spin. With supervision, of course."

"When do we leave?" Zed asked.

"Well..." said Beren slyly, "that's the best part. *We* don't."

"I've got far too many coronation preparations to finish, I couldn't possibly," said the Princess.

"I'm too old to be gallivanting around other dimensions," said Obaachan, turning toward Baba. "But a day trip to spoil some deserving children sounds like a perfect final exam for Grandma Boot Camp, don't you think?"

"We can make it a birthday outing," Baba agreed. "See the sights, collect samples of your favorite things Falinnheim is missing… maybe try this 'pizza' I've been hearing about."

"But of course you'll need a security escort," said the Princess. "Between Nyx and Lieutenant Solomon, I think you should be pretty well covered. You can set out first thing tomorrow morning, then we'll all meet back here at the end of the day for ice cream and cake. A *real* birthday cake," she added. "Chocolate, with rainbow sprinkles and thirteen candles."

"Thank you," said Tuesday at last. "It's perfect." Well, almost perfect, she realized. She looked down the table at her mother. "Can I make one more request?"

"Did we forget something?" Theadora asked.

"It's just… Iris's compasses belong to Gilford as much as they do to anybody. It's only fair he should get to finish what his grandmother started. And I could never describe the other Earth to the new Apprentice Librarian accurately enough. Bastian really should see it for himself. Can they come too?"

The Princess smiled. "It wouldn't be a proper birthday party without inviting a few friends."

———

Princess Theadora summoned Scrimbley back to the

palace, much to Tuesday and Baba's annoyance. In theory, Gilford had read enough about transporter compasses to set the coordinates himself. But everyone agreed that since Scrimbley was the only person in Falinnheim with firsthand experience using a compass, it was safer to let him be their interdimensional travel agent.

"I'll keep the control unit compass here with me," Scrimbley explained when the travelers assembled in the library the next morning. "One of you needs to keep the receiving compass in your pocket. Technically I can transport you back without it, but you'd have to be at the exact right coordinates—I believe it's calibrated for someplace in the woods?"

"The meeting tree!" Zed exclaimed. "I always wondered how you moved us here in the first place, since the receiving compass was with Mom and Dad. You had the coordinates to our treehouse?"

"Mighty clever thinking on your father's part," said Scrimbley. "He designed it as a kind of emergency exit. I can locate the receiving compass no matter where it is, but if things go sideways the treehouse is a good backup plan."

Princess Theadora gave the compass to Solomon, then handed Tuesday a stack of folded paper bills. "Luckily, I had some money with me when we came back to Falinnheim. It's useless here, so you may as well spend it on your trip. Should be enough to get you through a day back on the other Earth."

"Don't worry about a thing," Baba told Theadora and Beren. "We'll do our best to keep a low profile—just a little sightseeing. We'll be back before you know it."

Tuesday, Zed, Bastian, Gilford, Baba, and Solomon clustered together in the library entryway. Princess Theadora gave Nyx's ears a scritch, then sent the hound to sit at Baba's feet.

Scrimbley flipped open the compass lid and twiddled the dials. A blinding light enveloped the group, forcing everyone to close their eyes. And when they opened them again, they were standing in a patch of fresh spring undergrowth sprouting beneath a massive oak tree.

"That was *wild*," Bastian breathed. He craned his neck to look up at the treehouse. "I mean, I know this is what you expected, but I almost didn't believe it was going to work, you know?"

Tuesday grinned. "You haven't seen anything yet. Come on, let me show you around."

———

Everyone tromped through the woods until they reached the back porch of the Furst house. The doors and windows were all boarded up, and there was a big red sign nailed over the back door that read NO TRESPASSING.

"Good thing we're not trespassers," said Zed as Solomon and Gilford worked together to pry off the plywood covering and open the door. "It's our house, after all."

"Good luck explaining that to the cops if anybody notices," said Tuesday.

Inside, the house was just as they'd left it. Broken glass was strewn across some scorched patches in the carpet, evidence of Nyx's battle with the soldiers who had tried to kidnap Zed and Tuesday six months earlier. The electricity was turned off, but Baba and Solomon each pulled glass spheres from their pockets and lit them up like flashlights so Zed and Tuesday could see well enough to collect a few things from their old bedrooms.

Zed emptied the long-overdue school papers from his backpack and loaded it up with his favorite books. Tuesday collected the family photo album, her lucky polka-dotted socks, and Pinky Stiltskin, the plush flamingo that had been her favorite stuffed animal since she was four. (Bastian had absolutely no comment about this, much to Tuesday's relief.) Even Nyx got in on the act, digging through her toy basket for her favorite squeaky octopus and prancing proudly around the living room with her prize.

Tuesday also tried the kitchen, hoping to find an unopened jar of peanut butter in the pantry, but all the food had already been cleared out.

"Probably for the best," said Baba. "Whoever boarded up the windows probably didn't want things to spoil and attract pests."

After covering the door again and stashing their treasures at the base of the meeting tree, the next stop was the bus station. Solomon worried someone in town might recognize the kids or Nyx and start asking difficult questions, so they traveled to the next city over where they were less likely to bump into anyone they knew.

The bus driver didn't want to let Nyx on at first, but Zed insisted she was a service dog. (Which was true, mostly. She wasn't assisting with a disability, but security is a service, right?) Gilford and Bastian spent the twenty-minute bus ride marveling over all the cars they passed and drawing sketches of the local clothing fashions. They huddled together on the back row of the bus, whispering their observations like a couple of naturalists making a field guide to some uncharted wilderness.

Mostly the other bus passengers ignored them, except for a man dressed in ripped black jeans, sporting a purple mohawk. "Cool outfits," he said with an approving nod. "Ren Faire?"

Zed looked down at his brass tunic buttons and simple leather shoes. The rest of the group was dressed in Falinnheim fashions, too. No wonder the man thought they were headed to a medieval reenactment or something. "Rehearsing for a play," Zed fibbed.

"Rock on," said Mohawk Guy.

When they arrived in the city, they walked a lap of the historic district where all the fancy antique homes and government buildings sat. Solomon and Baba each used their glass spheres to record the view, documenting architecture styles, and Baba took a few plant cuttings from the shrubs planted along the sidewalk. Then they ducked into the old single-screen movie theater on Main Street, which was doing a free matinee of cartoons from the 1950s. Zed wasn't sure this was terribly educational for the Falinnheim-born members of the party, but at least it was fun. And most of the cartoons included classical music in the background, so that was something, right?

After leaving the theater, they wandered further down Main Street. Tuesday stared into the window of an electronics store they passed—maybe she could find a used cell phone or tablet and download some movies and music onto it? But then she realized it wouldn't be compatible with Falinnheim's crystal-powered energy grid. Once the phone's battery died, she'd have no way to recharge it. Falinnheim had screens too, but all the plugs and ports connecting them were different. Even if she took physical records like tapes or discs back with her, she didn't have the right devices to play them on. And if she took the devices, she couldn't make them connect to a screen.

Bastian tried to soothe her disappointment. "I guess we'll have to take paper records back with us, like Iris did. I mean, Zed's got an entire backpack full of books already, so we've made a good start."

"Don't worry about that," said Baba. "You'll never be able to document everything about the other Earth's culture and history for us newcomers. Just enjoy the day."

"Well I know what *I'd* enjoy," said Zed. "It's time to track down some lunch."

They found a pizza parlor on the next block, so Tuesday and Baba ordered pizzas and sodas to go, then joined everyone else in the park across the street.

"This is *amazing*," Bastian gushed when he tasted his first bite of pepperoni with extra cheese.

Gilford's lips puckered as he sipped his grape soda. "That tastes nothing like grapes," he declared. "And why is it so *sweet*?"

Zed found an abandoned Frisbee on a park bench, so after lunch they all spread out over the grass and took turns tossing it to each other. Everyone else had a bit of trouble with their aim, but Solomon was a natural. Nyx stationed herself in the middle and leapt up at every pass, trying to snatch the disc in midair.

After an hour they were all out of breath, so Tuesday suggested they spend the rest of the afternoon at the city library. Nyx had to wait outside this time, but that was fine. She was exhausted from all the Frisbee acrobatics anyway, so she curled up behind a bush outside the entrance and took a nap. Inside, Zed had a quick consultation with the librarian and reserved a study room with a computer. He and Tuesday spent the next three hours thinking up animals, plants, and inventions Falinnheim didn't have, then searching clips on YouTube that would explain them to the others.

"There has *got* to be a way to smuggle a kangaroo back to Falinnheim," Bastian joked. "Think they'll let us bring one on the bus?"

At last their computer reservation ended and it was time to head back to Falinnheim. But it seemed the library had one last gift for the explorers. Just inside the front door they found a wheeled cart stacked with old books the librarians had weeded from the catalog, marked FREE. Gilford chose an eight-volume set of children's encyclopedias, complete with color photographs of each entry. These days, kids who wanted to learn about elephants or bicycles or radio waves would probably use the internet. But for Gilford, who needed paper references to basic Other Earth information, the encyclopedias couldn't be more perfect. He didn't make a single complaint about hauling the heavy books all the way to the bus stop and spent the entire ride to the house browsing through them.

Bastian leaned over to whisper to Tuesday. "Looks like children's books are good enough for the Royal Librarian after all," he snickered.

The sun was sinking behind the horizon when they returned to the meeting tree. Solomon pulled the compass from his pocket and used a twig to inscribe the word HERE inside the lid. After a moment the etching dissolved and was replaced by a check mark.

"Looks like Scrimbley's ready for us," said Solomon.

"Everybody grab your things."

Everyone stood close together, arms full of their treasures. A blinding light appeared, then receded, and the next moment they were standing in the palace library.

"Welcome home," said Scrimbley.

Nyx shook herself off and trotted around the room, her tail wagging cheerfully and her mouth full of Squeaky Octopus. Everyone else dumped their things on the study tables and chatted among themselves about the day's adventures. But Tuesday just stood there, taking a moment to drink in the library's familiar scent and look over the happy group of her friends and family.

"Home," Tuesday repeated. She thought back to the abandoned, boarded-up house they'd just left, then looked down at the photo album clutched to her chest.

Things were different now. Only two days ago, she'd been desperate to get back to the other Earth, even if it meant sneaking off alone. But even if she'd succeeded, she could never truly go back to the way things were before. Her house was deserted and broken. She could never talk to her neighbors or school friends again without having to make up outrageous lies about where she'd been. She could never return to her childhood ignorance, before she learned how complicated and dangerous and *weird* the world truly was. And yet, she realized with a surge of pride, she'd fought her way through the challenges of the past few months. And because of those challenges, she understood better than ever what she was capable of and what really mattered to her.

It was the comfort and security of her past that she missed, not the house or the town. Sure, she'd spent her entire childhood complaining Mom and Dad were up to something, but she'd never doubted that they loved her and wanted the best for her. Zed and Nyx, too. No family was perfect, but even with its flaws, hers was something special. And now that they'd been reunited with Baba and Obaachan, it was better than ever.

Tuesday had all the time in the world to build new memories. And the old ones would always be part of her, even if she couldn't return to them.

"It's good to be back," she told Scrimbley. "Now—let's go have some cake!"

CHAPTER 24
OOPS

The moment he heard the word "cake", Scrimbley set off for the dining room. Baba hurried after him, probably to make sure he didn't get "lost" along the way and start pocketing valuables. Gilford followed her, anxious to report his Other Earth research to the Princess. That left Solomon to escort the kids and Nyx downstairs to rejoin the party.

"Where is everybody?" Zed asked as they passed through the silent, deserted hallways. At this time of evening the palace would normally be a hive of activity, with all the village liaison employees closing up their offices and the maids and porters changing shifts. But every room they passed was dark and empty.

"I hear Obaachan gave the entire staff the day off," Solomon explained. "Even the chef. Apparently, your mother insisted on making the birthday cake herself."

Perhaps if the palace hadn't been so quiet, they wouldn't have noticed what happened next. Or perhaps the unusual stillness and solitude was the reason it happened at all. Either way, the entire group paused and listened as they rounded the corner to the second-floor stairwell. Snatches of hushed conversation emerged from a dimmed office down the hall. Irregular pulses of green light spilled from the half-open door in a way that reminded Tuesday of walking past a dark room where a TV was on.

Nyx's ears perked up. She spit out Squeaky Octopus and padded toward the door to investigate. The hound's suspicion caught Solomon's attention, so he flattened his back to the wall and eased closer.

Two men were talking.

"No one will suspect a thing."

"How soon can we act?"

"The warden said the compass was delivered to the palace this morning. I'm keeping an eye out for it, but if I can't access it here it will be returned to the jail soon anyway, and Grimsbee can get it there."

"We have to time this carefully. If we move the night after the warden's scheduled inspection, it could be a full week before anyone knows I'm missing. That would give us time to assemble the missing agents."

Zed, Tuesday, and Bastian tiptoed behind Solomon and peeked through the doorway. From this angle it was impossible to see who was speaking, but they definitely had one of the palace's new hologram projectors turned on—the green light was unmistakable.

Nyx moved to the center of the hall to get a better viewing angle. Over Solomon's mimed objections, Tuesday followed her.

It wasn't two men. Well, it was, but only one of them was really there. A middle-aged man in a porter's uniform stood leaning against a desk, facing a hologram projector. And beaming from the floor in a column of flickering, green-tinged light was none other than Tyrren.

Nyx growled. Tuesday scrambled backward to avoid the blue flames igniting along the hound's back. Solomon drew a long knife from his belt holster and nudged the door the rest of the way open. "Downstairs," he ordered the children. "Now."

<hr>

Princess Theadora and Captain Beren charged up the stairs two at a time just as Tuesday, Zed, and Bastian were scrambling down. They met in the middle of the first-floor staircase, where Zed tried to explain. "Tyrren," he panted, "but it's a hologram—there's a spy in the palace, and—"

"I saw," was all the Princess said. "Nyx." She pointed him toward the dining room and continued up the stairs.

By the time the kids made it to the dining room and filled in the rest of the adults, they had calmed down considerably. Tyrren wasn't really here, after all. And between Solomon's old-fashioned combat skills, Beren's slipsteel weapon, and the Princess directing Nyx, the spy would be arrested with no trouble.

"You've got to admit, seeing Nyx go all Flame Mode was pretty awesome," Bastian added. "I was starting to wonder if the Gabriel Hound legends were exaggerated. All I ever saw was normal dog stuff."

"She's sneaky like that," said Zed. "It took us years to catch her in the act."

"Ain't nothin normal about that beast," said Scrimbley. "It's lucky I haven't found myself on her bad side yet."

"Let's keep it that way," said Baba.

Tuesday described the man in the office to Obaachan, who said he'd been hired as a kitchen porter only the previous week. "A Red Hand agent," she assumed. "Probably wanted to pass palace gossip to a contact at Alexandria's jail. They'd have tried to break Tyrren out if we hadn't sent him Elsewhere. The porter must have seen the guards testing out the new hologram system and taught Tyrren how to modify his holographic counselor to pull off the same trick."

"I *knew* it!" Bastian blurted. "I told you they'd programmed him a psychiatrist!"

"Doesn't matter," Tuesday grumped. "Freud himself couldn't talk Tyrren out of dreaming up evil plots."

"Who's Freud?" asked Gilford.

"Check your encyclopedia," said Zed, who was too worked up to explain the reference.

———

Obaachan insisted they couldn't cut the cake until Theadora, Beren, and Solomon could join them. And since they had to turn the shackled spy over to the jail warden, file evidence reports, and figure out who Grimsbee was so they could arrest him too, it was likely to be a while. So Baba returned the cake to the refrigerator, and everyone accepted Gilford's invitation to the staff dinner instead.

"I guess we'll let it slide just this once," Bastian teased Tuesday as they followed Gilford down the service stairwell. "After all, it is your birthday."

Tuesday hesitated in the doorway. The rest of the group filed in and joined the buffet line. No one seemed to notice them, much less object to the intrusion. The long table was already filling up with people laughing and chatting and passing around salt and pepper shakers. There were no uniforms to tell who worked in which department, since they'd all dressed casually for their day off. Bastian waved to his parents, who smiled and pointed enthusiastically at a cluster of empty seats near theirs.

The room was hot. And noisy. And crowded. And cheerful.

It was perfect, Tuesday decided.

CHAPTER 25
THE NEXT CHAPTER

This proved it, the Princess's advisors agreed. Even the jail warden was convinced. Tyrren was simply too dangerous to keep locked up.

They'd captured two members of the Red Hand, but there was no telling how many were still out there. It didn't matter where they put Tyrren's prison. If the guards knew where to check on him, eventually the Red Hand would find a way to do the same.

The only solution, it seemed, was not to imprison him at all.

Theadora said she got the idea while reading a story. Her own story, as a matter of fact, which she was typing up to add to *The Book of the Founders*. She'd managed to avoid Tyrren's spies for sixteen years by traveling to the other Earth. And in the end, the plan only failed because someone in Falinnheim knew where to find her. She wouldn't be repeating that mistake.

Gilford searched the archive and found a list of transporter coordinates. He copied the coordinates down without labeling them, and Beren chose one at random. Scrimbley used Iris's compass to transport Tyrren from his exile in Elsewhere to the Alexandria jail, just for a second. The jail warden confiscated the hologram projector from Tyrren's luggage. Then Scrimbley entered the new coordinates, transporting Tyrren and all his supplies to the other Earth.

Scrimbley reset the dials on the compass, then handed it to the Princess, who reset them again. Since they didn't send him with a compass, Tyrren could never return to Falinnheim. And since neither Scrimbley, Gilford, Beren, or even the Princess knew where he'd ended up, the Red Hand would never know either.

Tuesday had to admit it was a creative solution, when her parents explained everything later. "But it's hardly a fair punishment, considering all the terrible things he's done," she argued.

Zed was all for creative solutions, but even he thought Tuesday had a point.

"Mom and I know that better than anyone," said Beren. "His crimes were against our families, after all. But maybe it's time we started looking forward, instead of backward. Finding solutions that prevent future problems, rather than avenging the past. Besides, Tyrren's unquenchable ambition started all this in the first place. He couldn't handle living in a society he didn't control. Having to start over in a world where he has no control over anyone, with no power and no followers, is the worst punishment Tyrren can imagine."

"Your father's right," said Baba. "Tyrren's obsession with control caused sixteen years of chaos. We can't fall into the same trap he did. Trying to control Tyrren might feel like justice, but it will never bring peace. The only way to break this cycle is to let go."

"I'm not foolish enough to think a fresh start will change Tyrren's nature," Theadora concluded. "But at least whatever happens next will be his choice. And the consequences will be his responsibility."

"Speaking of responsibility," said Baba, frowning at Zed and Tuesday, "Gilford informs me the excitement of the last few days has put you behind in your schoolwork."

Tuesday groaned.

"Mind your manners," Theadora warned. "Your grandmother's absolutely right. You and Zed have assignments to catch up on." She reached into her handbag and withdrew a massive book, which she handed sternly to Tuesday.

Tuesday rolled her eyes and stuffed the book into her school bag. But then she noticed Obaachan's mischievous grin and decided she'd better actually look at it.

The midnight-blue cover. The silver lettering. The twin raven emblem. It was *The Book of the Founders.*

"I believe Gilford assigned his students to read this," said the Princess, maintaining her mock-serious tone. "You and Zed better get caught up so you can let Bastian take his turn. And when you're done, I have a new assignment for you. My advisors agreed the book won't be complete until you and Zed add your story to it. And there's a lot to tell, with all the wild adventures you've been on this year. We might have to publish an entire second volume to fit it all in."

"Sorry," Zed interrupted, "did you say *publish*?"

"After listening to an impassioned speech from the Royal Librarian, I decided the grand opening of the Falinnheim Historical Archive has been put off long enough. Construction on a museum in downtown Alexandria starts next week. But naturally we can't expect everyone interested in Falinnheim's history to travel to the capitol. When Gilford is done writing Iris's story, and you and Zed finish yours, we'll print an updated edition of *The Book of the Founders* and donate a copy to every library, school, and village council in Falinnheim."

"These advisors of yours sound pretty smart," said Tuesday. "Maybe joining the Regents Council someday won't be so bad after all."

"You've got plenty of time left to decide," her mother answered. "I think you'd do a fantastic job on the council. But if some other profession catches your eye, that's fine, too."

Zed could hardly believe his ears. "Really?" he asked, beaming. "What changed your mind?"

His father laughed. "Obaachan might have had something to say about that. She pointed out how ironic it was to let our worst enemy choose the next chapter in his life but deny that choice to our own children."

"I might also have threatened to get Shinbiter involved," Obaachan joked, patting her walking stick fondly.

Tuesday had no idea what sort of job she might choose for her apprenticeship. The realization that she had only two years left to come up with something suddenly felt rather heavy. But even with the pressure of a deadline, she was glad to know the choice was hers to make, in the end.

Zed was busy thinking, too. "Borrowing Dad's umbrella last winter taught me a lot," he said. "But I've still got a ton of questions about how slipsteel works. Do you think, if we ever find the missing steelsmith, I could study with them?"

"You'd make an excellent steelsmith's apprentice," the Princess declared.

"What about your council, though?" asked Tuesday. "I mean, you've been pulling Dad, Gilford, and Obaachan into meetings all week, but they've got their own jobs to do. And Baba is heading back to the base after the coronation. If Zed and I don't ever join the Regents Council, you'll be stuck deciding everything alone again."

"I've still got the village liaison office," she said. "They keep pretty good tabs on the needs and priorities of each town. But you're right, we need a more permanent solution. Basing decisions on one person's whims never ends well."

Tuesday stared thoughtfully at the book in her hands. The silver ravens glinted at her from the cover. When she first read Olav's story, she assumed the royal crest evolved from the viking's fondness for the birds. But perhaps there was more to it. The way they stood, facing opposite directions, keeping watch both forward and back… it was almost as if they were staring into the past and the future.

Iris had been good at that. Her predictions about the Regents Council had been scarily accurate. The Regents Council spent centuries falling into the same trap that destroyed the first Library of Alexandria—an obsession with power and controlling information. They hadn't learned from the mistakes of the past, so they'd repeated them when planning what came next.

It's too bad Iris wasn't here. She'd make the perfect addition to Mom's council.

But maybe, if they couldn't have Iris, they could have the next best thing…

"People already vote for their mayors and village councils," Tuesday reasoned aloud. "But if they elected members of the Regents Council too, some of them would probably end up being like Tyrren—people who love being in charge, and will do whatever it takes to get there. What we really need are people who understand the lessons from stories, and help others find the right story for their situation. People who are good at organizing information and listening to the members of their community."

"That sounds perfect," said the Princess. "You know anybody like that?"

Tuesday grinned. "I think I might."

———

One week later, Tuesday and Zed stood in the capitol square, facing the biggest crowd they had ever seen. Tuesday still wasn't a fan of her green dress, but she tried to ignore the itchy ribbons and pay attention to her mother's coronation speech. Instead of being named Queen or Empress or some equally fancy upgrade on Princess, Theadora had decided to take the title of Moderator.

Her first act as Moderator was to announce the formation of the Ambassador Librarians Program. Librarians from all over Falinnheim were invited to apply for a one-year term on the Regents Council. Twenty would be chosen to advise the Moderator, and the rest would participate in an exchange program to cover the advisors' jobs while they were away. Each year, they'd select a new group. That way none of the librarians had to leave a job they loved for very long, and none would stay in the capitol so long they lost touch with the problems and priorities of the people back home. After all, Theadora reminded the cheering crowd, Falinnheim was founded by a librarian. Who better to keep it on the right track?

After the parades and speeches were done, it was time

to return to the palace. The coronation banquet was still to come, but that was hours away. "There will always be time for work," Obaachan insisted. "Right now, we've got a birthday party to finish."

They'd eaten the birthday cake days ago, of course. But Zed and Bastian had insisted they needed more time to plan the party game. After days spent feverishly scribbling on note cards and scouring the palace cupboards for props, they were finally ready to unveil their invention: a life-sized version of an Other Earth board game, using the palace's rooms and secret passageways as their playing field.

"First," Zed explained, "everyone needs to choose a character." He dug through a bin of costumes and pulled out a yellow jacket. "Who wants to be Colonel Mustard?"

Baba frowned uncertainly. Dressing up in costumes and acting things out wasn't her idea of a good time, she complained. But solving a mystery sounded okay. She finally agreed to play along, but only because Obaachan refused to let her graduate from Grandma Boot Camp if she tried to get out of it.

"Come on," Bastian urged her, showing off the various hats and scarves. "You can be anyone you want."

Tuesday smiled. Bastian was right. With Falinnheim entering its new era, they could all choose who they wanted to be. She couldn't predict how everything might turn out, but those chapters could wait. For now, she'd focus on one decision at a time.

Tuesday pulled an oversized purple vest from the costume pile and waved it overhead. "I call Professor Plum!"

www.ingramcontent.com/pod-product-compliance
Lightning Source LLC
Chambersburg PA
CBHW061525210726
48287CB00006B/1832